ELECTRIFY
HIS HEART

ALANA ANKH

Dreamspinner Press

Published by
DREAMSPINNER PRESS

5032 Capital Circle SW, Suite 2, PMB# 279, Tallahassee, FL 32305-7886 USA
http://www.dreamspinnerpress.com/

Electrify His Heart
© 2014 Alana Ankh.

Cover Art
© 2014 Paul Richmond.
www.paulrichmondstudio.com
Cover content is for illustrative purposes only and any person depicted on the cover is a model.

ISBN: 978-1-62798-963-3
Digital ISBN: 978-1-62798-964-0
Library of Congress Control Number: 2014944016
First Edition September 2014

Printed in the United States of America
∞
This paper meets the requirements of
ANSI/NISO Z39.48-1992 (Permanence of Paper).

Prologue

January 1, 2441

LUCIUS HARTMAN lay on the hospital platform, patiently waiting for the scan to be completed. The sensors strapped to him beeped rhythmically as they registered his pulse, his breathing, and of course, the functionality of his implants. As the machine scrambled his mental computer, he winced but said nothing.

"Sorry about that," his friend and doctor, Hugh Wells, said.

"It's all right," Lucius replied. "Not your fault. Some unpleasantness can't be helped."

The medical check was compulsory for everyone with a cybernetic coefficient—or CC—over 50 percent. Procedures were far safer now than in the twenty-second century, when scientists finally uncovered the procedure that allowed man to safely replace his organs with cybernetic implants. However, Lucius was very much aware that exchanging his formerly human body for a stronger cyborg one came with consequences. His CC—the percentage of tech he'd managed to absorb into his flesh—made him a better soldier, but that didn't mean he could blind himself to the risks. He had children to worry about, so he needed to be careful.

At last the checkup ended and the scanners stopped their beeping. Hugh stepped up from his seat and started to remove the sensors. "Well, Doc?" Lucius asked. "Do I get a clean bill of health?"

Hugh snorted. "You know you do, you old dog. I still have no idea how you do it. One of these days, you're going to have to tell me your secret."

"I'd rather not," Lucius replied. "There are enough high-CC cyborgs as it is."

His friend shook his head. "I always wonder about you, Lucius. You worry so much about the effects of implants, and yet…."

"I did what I had to do, Hugh," Lucius answered seriously. "Anyway, thank you for the help."

Hugh cleared his throat, obviously understanding the dismissal of the conversation. "I take it you'll be going on a mission soon."

"Probably. Mr. Phelps called me in for one of his… conversations."

He never discussed what he actually had to do for the magnate, and Hugh knew better than to ask. "All right, then." His friend squeezed Lucius's shoulder. "Say hi to the kids for me, and remind Raze he's due for a checkup too."

Lucius grimaced but nodded. His teenage son was nothing if not stubborn, but he'd have to obey him in this. "Will do. Bye, Hugh."

Hugh waved at him, and Lucius left the medical room, both relieved and burdened by the knowledge of another medical checkup successfully passed. He didn't know why, but for years he'd felt like he lived with the proverbial Sword of Damocles hanging over his head. He'd been forced to embrace that, because otherwise, he'd never have been able to make a living as a soldier, but that didn't mean he was happy with it.

He took the elevator to the ground floor, distantly registering the voice of the AI that reminded all high-CC cyborgs to come in for their checkup. Behind him, someone grumbled as he scrolled through his newspaper tablet. "I just knew we should have never given up nuclear energy. These solar cells are going to kill us."

Lucius ignored the other man and stepped out of the elevator. According to his mental computer, it was almost noon, which meant his sons had been left alone and unsupervised for almost half an hour. The mischief Raze and Julian could get into in that kind of time somewhat horrified him.

Thankfully, Lucius found his sons waiting patiently outside. Raze leaned against their hovercraft, talking in a low voice with his best friend, Logan Maxfield. At one point, he'd captured a service drone, which he'd given to Julian to play with.

Julian poked the tiny robot disinterestedly—he'd never been as attracted to taking things apart as Raze—and looked up at his older brother with yearning. Raze stopped midsentence, turned toward his brother, and ruffled his hair. "Bored? Don't worry. Father will be here soon, and then we can go to the space park."

"I'm here now," Lucius intervened.

Julian squealed in delight, launching himself at Lucius, a tiny ball of energy and enthusiasm. Lucius picked his youngest up with ease, his heart clenching as he took in Julian's delicate face. Both his sons looked so much like Anne Marie it hurt—Julian even more so than Raze—and in moments such as these, Lucius wished so badly that she could have been there to see them grow. But since Anne Marie's death, Lucius had been raising his sons on his own, and for that reason, he couldn't bring himself to regret sacrificing his humanity. At least the boys would always have a father to protect them.

"Hey, Jules," he said to his youngest. "Did you get bored?"

Julian just shrugged, as unwilling to complain as always. Lucius chuckled. He turned toward Logan, who greeted him politely.

"Hello, Mr. Hartman."

"Hey, kiddo. You're here with your folks?"

Logan nodded. "They're in for their checkup too. After that, they promised to get me one of those new VR engines."

"Father, can we get a VR engine?" Julian asked. "Logan says it's really awesome."

"Stop feeding my son nonsense," Lucius mock-chastised Logan. He kissed Julian's forehead and added, "Virtual reality isn't for kids your age, Jules."

"Why not?" Julian pouted. "He says they can make it snow in VR. I want to see snow."

That wasn't the only thing people could do in virtual reality engines, which was why impressionable seven-year-olds were forbidden to access them. "You will, Jules," Lucius promised, "just not right now."

Raze cleared his throat, interrupting the moment. "Everything okay?" he inquired quietly.

"Of course. You know me. As healthy as a horse." He paused, shooting his son a serious glance. "But you have to go in too."

"I will," Raze promised. "Just… not right now."

Anger swelled through Lucius, hot and bright. His son always enjoyed turning his words against him, and while as a rule Lucius accepted it with a smile, he wanted Raze to acknowledge the dangers of the choice he was making. "This isn't a joke, Raze. Your cybernetic coefficient is something you need to take very seriously. It's not solely about getting the implants. It also depends on how they bond with your body."

"I'll be fine, Father," Raze replied, "and I said I would go. I just don't want to waste today on it. Okay?"

Lucius's shoulders slumped. He couldn't argue with Raze, not when his son asked so little of him. He was away so much because of his work, and sometimes it truly felt like both Raze and Julian had grown up in the blink of an eye. Sacrificing those precious years he could have spent at their side hurt him more than becoming half machine ever could.

"Fair enough. I do believe I promised you boys a visit to the space park."

4

Julian clapped his hands excitedly, although Lucius had to wonder if his youngest son was simply happy about getting to spend time with his father. Lucius knew exactly how he felt. He passed Julian to Raze and ushered them both into the hovercraft.

Raze said his good-byes to Logan, and just like that, they were off. Traffic seemed particularly wicked today, the various highways cluttered with aircrafts big and small. Lucius grimaced when he caught sight of a nuclear-powered one. Those things were a recipe for disaster in big cities. Perhaps after this job, he'd be able to make enough money to move from the capital to somewhere Julian and Raze could grow up without worry.

That was the last thought Lucius had before his mental computer shut down. The world went black, and Lucius knew no more.

IN THE very same hospital Lucius Hartman had left not ten minutes earlier, chaos erupted. Every single piece of equipment short-circuited and died. Hugh Wells clutched his head and screamed, collapsing on the floor and twitching wildly. Nurses and doctors all slid to the ground, crumpling among the now useless service drones.

In the maternity ward, babies who had been born that day cried for a single instant and then went perfectly still. A sole baby boy kept crying, his big green eyes filling with fat tears as he took in the destruction he didn't understand. Around him, silence fell where once had been the hum of electricity and machines, broken only by the distant sound of explosions and screams.

Chapter One

March 3, 2461, somewhere in the outskirts of Genesis, capital city of Eden

SCOTT CARRIED *Eric to the bedroom and placed him on the mattress. He followed Eric down and covered his lover's body with his own. He brought their dicks together and engulfed them in his hand. As they kissed, they moved against each other, their cocks still slick with cum. The feel of Eric's dick against his made passion pulse inside Scott. He considered making Eric climax just by using his hand or his mouth but decided against it. He wanted this night to last. After all, it had been far too difficult to steal these moments together, and every second was precious.*

Eric rubbed against him, and somehow Scott could hear his lover gasp and moan even with their mouths molded together. Scott found that even if he'd just taken Eric minutes ago, he wanted to be inside Eric again.

"Yes, God, Scott, yes," Eric begged.

Scott distantly realized he'd at some point separated their mouths, but he couldn't for his life fathom what had possessed him to do so. Not even breathing could be more important than kissing, tasting his lover.

He didn't waste any time in complying with Eric's request. He placed his dick at Eric's opening and pushed. Eric's passage was already slick and stretched, so Scott easily slid in. As sensations hit them both, Eric gasped softly and clung to Scott's neck.

Scott kept his gaze fixed on Eric's eyes, greedily taking in every emotion passing through the deep green orbs. He started moving slowly, thrusting in and out of Eric's passage, taking his time, savoring the feel of Eric's body around him.

It felt like home. Safe, loved, but so intense at the same time. Scott had never thought something like this was possible before meeting Eric. His beautiful lover made it possible. Eric had given him emotions, awakened his dead, dark heart.

Scott kept his motions as gentle and soft as a spring breeze, his heart swelling with love and his body finding perfection in their union. The passion was still there, but beyond that, their minds and souls acknowledged how much they needed each other. Through their link, they felt things double, or rather, they were finally complete.

Eric moved with him, meeting Scott thrust for thrust. As their bodies connected in the most intimate way possible, Scott had the random thought that it was an echo of their very souls becoming one.

Eric's lips beckoned him forward, and Scott didn't resist their temptation. As they kissed once again, Scott felt the need in both their bodies grow to irrepressible proportions. He instinctively started thrusting harder inside Eric, and his lover pushed back, impaling himself on Scott's dick. Their bodies moved in tandem, their very hearts following the same rhythm. God.... Scott could never get tired of fucking Eric, of being balls deep inside him.

URIEL BIT his lip and gasped slightly as he took in the scandalous words on the paper. The old volume hadn't been easy to acquire.

He'd found it by accident, in the library. He could only guess that it must have belonged to someone else before, but it was so ancient that the ink had started to fade. Still, he could distinguish what had been written—and it was far more intense than his wildest dreams or anything he could have ever imagined throughout his lonely nights. He didn't dare to touch himself, because he knew it would be wrong, but he could easily see himself in the main character's place. To feel the heat of someone kissing him, caressing him, touching him in his most intimate places.... To have a say in what he wanted, to be seen as a lover, not as an object.... It was unbelievable even as a fantasy.

He was so engrossed in the story that he lost track of his surroundings. When the door to his quarters opened, Uriel jumped guiltily and snapped the book shut. He tried to hide it under his hair, hoping that whoever had entered his room wouldn't think of looking for the item there. Sadly, the intruder in question had no such limitations.

His mother burst into his bedroom, already seeming in a bad mood. "What are you doing, Uriel? Get dressed. The Council is arriving in half an hour, and you still haven't combed your hair."

Uriel blinked at her but didn't leave the bed. It wasn't unusual for him to spend some time resting like this, in his private quarters, with the fire burning in the hearth. She would think nothing of it. "Is the Council visiting?" he asked.

His mother rolled her eyes at him. "Have you forgotten what day it is tomorrow?"

Uriel scanned his memory for what she could be referring to. Half the time he couldn't keep track of the passing of days. For him, they were pretty much identical. He woke up, studied, trained, bathed, then went to bed. Sometimes, if he got lucky, he had some free time, which, as a rule, he spent reading. The highlight of his past year had been finding this particular book—which he imagined must have been an accident of sorts. His mother would have never allowed him in the library if she'd known there was such a tome there.

Had he forgotten about something important because he was so lost in the world of fantasy? He must have, because otherwise his mother wouldn't have been so frustrated with him.

And then it hit him. Of course. Tomorrow would be one of *those* days. His stomach roiled as he finally remembered why the Council had decided to visit his so-called home. He must have subconsciously pushed it to the back of his mind because the entire process was so repulsive for him.

Uriel couldn't explain that to his mother, though. "I apologize," he said softly. "I'll start getting ready now."

Unfortunately, as he moved, his book tangled in his long hair instead of innocuously remaining next to the pillows. When he slid out of the bed, it fell to the floor. Of course his mother noticed at once. Uriel picked it up before she could do so, but she reached his side in seconds, extending her palm. "Show me what you have there."

Uriel's heart fell, and he cursed himself for his stupidity and his clumsiness. Normally his ruse with the hair would have worked, but today, because of his distraction, it had backfired on him. Uriel could already tell his mother had noticed the explicit cover, but even if she hadn't, she made it her business to check over everything Uriel read—which was why he'd hidden the book from her in the first place.

"Uriel, give it to me," she insisted.

Uriel shook his head. He knew that if he did so he'd never get it back. It might have been petty and foolish, but he wanted to finish the story of Scott and Eric. He wanted to see them in his mind's eye, holding each other and smiling together. If Uriel would never have that, he could at least get a glimpse of it in the happiness between the lines written in faded ink.

But his mother had other ideas. Moving faster than the eye could see, she snatched the tome from Uriel and scanned the cover with visible distaste.

Uriel berated himself for not paying more attention to her actions. She was one of the cyborgs with a 30 percent cybernetic coefficient that had survived the virus. She'd removed the implants a long time ago through a procedure that had nearly killed her. Now she still trained on a regular basis to keep her body in top physical shape, almost like she wanted to reach the performances she had when she'd been a cyborg. Uriel trained too since his duties required it, but she could easily defeat him with two well-placed kicks. At least, hypothetically speaking—because in reality, it was illegal to strike him. She had other ways to express her displeasure.

"Where did you get this book?" Uriel's mother scowled at him as she flipped through the pages of the volume. She grimaced in disapproval when she caught sight of a certain paragraph. "Guiding Light Uriel Noah of the House of Zion, answer the question. Where did you get this volume filled with such perversion?"

"It's a romance story, Mother," he replied rebelliously. "Why is it okay for me to pass through the ceremony when I can't even read a romance story?"

His mother's face grew red with fury. Undoubtedly, she wanted to hit him, but in spite of her role as Uriel's Guardian, she couldn't go against the law. "Remember your position, Uriel. Don't you dare compare such a religious process with pleasures of the flesh. Imagine what would happen if anyone even heard you say these things."

"So let them hear!" Uriel shouted back. "I'm not ashamed of it."

With an angry snarl, his mother stalked to the fireplace and tossed the book inside. The tome went up in flames, much like everything Uriel ever wanted and ever dreamed. He instinctively reached for it, but his mother held him back before he could burn himself.

"Get a hold of yourself, Uriel," she said. "Can't you see what you're doing? You are our Guiding Light. You're above all of these things. I realize that at times the responsibility is hard for you to bear, but you were given this gift because you can carry the burden that comes with it."

Uriel's heart fell. As much as he hated to admit it, she was right. The virus that had swept over their entire world had killed all newborns, save for him. He had lived, enduring the apocalypse that had decimated most of the cyborgs with high cybernetic coefficients.

"You survived the virus for a reason, Uriel," his mother continued to rant. "You were meant to guide us. You allowed us to rebuild, to heal our wounded world. How can you forget that for something so trivial?"

It was all true. The country previously known as the United States had changed into what was now Eden—a land built around Uriel, around the Guiding Light that had become humanity's last beacon of hope. It didn't matter that Uriel hated his role. His mother didn't care about his opinions and desires. No one did. This whole argument was stupid and pathetic, and Uriel felt like a child for clinging to such a little thing, when the entire world relied on him to be its pillar.

"I apologize, Mother," he said with a tight smile. "I don't know what came over me."

In response, she finally released her hold on him. "It's all right," she soothed Uriel. "It's not your fault. I've told the Council to be stricter with the regulations on these things. They're very dangerous, especially for you but also for the general populace. It's unfortunate, but I'll have to make note of this episode."

"I'm sure whatever you decide is best, Mother," Uriel answered. Still, he felt uncomfortable with the idea of having the people deprived of the written word because of his inability to accept the burden he had to carry. Licking his lips, he said, "I would dare to make one small request. I'd prefer it if the Council didn't find out about this one moment of weakness."

His mother hummed thoughtfully. "Well, I suppose you're right in that it would be quite embarrassing. Very well, as long as I have your word it won't happen again. No more books, Uriel."

Uriel swallowed around the sudden knot in his throat. She was taking away the one escape he had from his cage. But it had been only a matter of time, and he needed to accept it. He had to stop being Uriel and just be the Guiding Light, like they wanted.

"I understand," he told her. "No more books."

She beamed in smug satisfaction and patted Uriel's shoulder in a gesture that might have seemed motherly if he hadn't known any better. "Excellent. Now come. Let me comb your hair and get you ready."

His mother sat him down in front of the mirror and picked up his brush. While Uriel had been lying in bed, his hair had grown a little tangled, but it wasn't anything worrisome, because almost at every hour of the day he had servants hovering, ready to mend anything that would keep his physique from being flawless. To this day, Uriel wondered how they managed to do so without making contact with his skin. Only on the eve of the ceremonies did his mother step in herself, since she wanted everything to be perfect.

Uriel sat there looking at his reflection in the mirror and trying not to think about what he was getting ready for. With every day that passed, his role as a Guiding Light weighed on him more and more. He felt like he was missing something important. He was supposed to be the man who led the rest of the world to create a peaceful society. But how could he do that when his eyes were blind to what happened outside these walls and his ears deaf to everyone except the Council? Surely the fight for peace and prosperity went beyond these ceremonial days he hated so much.

Alas, complaining would be absolutely useless. In a way, Uriel had chosen his own entrapment. He dreaded the days when he actually had to open his eyes, because it meant having to face this role he loathed beyond measure. He preferred hiding here—and if only for that, he needed to show some courage when it was expected of him.

His mother combed his hair patiently, carefully, almost lovingly. When she was done with that, she braided it into a tight, formal knot. Due to the length of his locks, it would never hold, but it didn't have to—not beyond the meeting with the Council. Humming in approval, she then went to his wardrobe and found an elegant outfit inside. Intricately handwoven with symbols of their house, it was nonetheless far simpler than what Uriel would be wearing during the actual ceremony—or at least during a part of it.

Uriel put on the chosen garment without a word. His mother didn't leave the room, but he was used to that. He couldn't afford shyness given what his role as a Guiding Light entailed. His body didn't belong to him, and he'd long ago gotten used to that fact. He could have never survived otherwise.

His mother had already started glancing at the clock and sighing in frustration. She didn't actually rush him, but he got the message just the same. Fortunately, Uriel didn't have to brave her displeasure again, because it was only when he'd finished preparations that a knock sounded at the door.

"Yes?" Uriel's mother called out. "Come in."

The butler in charge of Uriel's so-called home, a man named Phelps, entered the room and bowed lowly. "Your Holiness," he said, glancing at Uriel longingly, "the Council has arrived."

Phelps had once been a very important businessman, but after the virus his financial empire had crumbled overnight, as had all of his implants. Now he stuck by Uriel's side because, according to him, Uriel helped him soothe the wounds of his past.

"Thank you, Phelps," Uriel replied with a soft smile.

As his mother started to guide him out of the room, Phelps hesitated slightly. "What is it?" Uriel asked, guessing he had something in mind.

"With your permission, might I be allowed to come to the ceremony tomorrow?"

To a certain extent, Uriel wasn't surprised that the man had asked. He'd never come before, largely because, at his age, the entire process would be demanding. "I would not keep you from it," Uriel answered, "but you must promise to be careful."

"I will, Your Holiness," the butler replied, smiling slightly. "Thank you. May you forever be blessed for your generosity."

His mother released a sound of impatience and finally took Uriel's arm. She couldn't physically force him out of the room, not with someone else around, but he knew resisting her would just make things worse.

With a final nod to the butler, Uriel abandoned his quarters. Servants bowed down to him as he walked, making him even more aware of the responsibility he carried. Uriel smiled and murmured blessings to each of them, and some of them actually broke down in tears.

"See?" his mother whispered in Uriel's ear. "They need you to be like this. You can't falter, Uriel. Imagine what would happen if you do."

"I understand, Mother," he replied. "Like I said, it won't happen again."

He'd made a serious mistake. Uriel realized that now. As the Guiding Light, he couldn't afford free time and hobbies. That sort of thing was for people. He couldn't have them, and he needed to stop wanting them, because it would only hurt more when it became obvious that they would forever be an unattainable dream.

When they reached the living room of his home, Uriel found the Council already waiting. The head councilman, Ezekiel Zion, bowed slightly at Uriel. "Are you ready, Your Holiness?"

Once more, Uriel forced a smile. Coincidentally, Ezekiel was also his father, but they didn't have that kind of relationship. For Ezekiel, Uriel had no worth as a son, just as the Guiding Light. He and Uriel's mother were still married, but they didn't live together either. None of them actually belonged to a family, beyond sharing the same last name, that of the House of Zion.

Uriel didn't bother approaching the man in a father-son way. "Yes, Head Councilman Ezekiel," he answered serenely. "I am."

"I'm sure you must be very excited," the other man said. "You haven't been in Genesis for quite some time. I know you have been missed at the temple."

"Genesis will always be my home," Uriel replied, "but I like it here too. I appreciate the affection and loyalty I've received from everyone here."

The Temple of Genesis was the place where Uriel had grown up. As a child, he'd learned the truth about his identity from Genesis priests.

Then, as more and more people gathered around the temple, Genesis had grown into an outright metropolis. The cyborgs had become increasingly resentful, creating a sort of resistance that threatened Uriel's life. It had then become obvious that the temple could no longer guarantee Uriel's safety. Upon Uriel's eighteenth birthday, the Council had sent him away to the special underground compound where he now lived.

He should have looked forward to ceremonial days, because it was the only time he got to leave the compound. Instead, he'd grown to dread them—because he was expected to shine brighter than the sun and moon put together.

But of course, he couldn't say anything like that, so instead he added, "Perhaps we should go. I believe there's a long way ahead of us, and tomorrow will be a busy day."

Outside, several carriages were already waiting. Uriel's was pulled by four white horses and bore the mark of the House of Zion. It would take him from the compound into the city. Uriel slid inside without another word, with his mother and his... father getting in after him. A group of mounted guards surrounded their little caravan. After all, the safety of the Guiding Light never ceased to be a priority.

Suppressing a sigh, Uriel settled in while watching the scenery go past. This part of Eden had been left untainted by civilization. There was only green grass as far as the eye could see. The entire territory supposedly belonged to Uriel, but he'd never once stepped outside to feel the blades of grass underneath his bare feet. Right then and there, it didn't seem like he ever would.

Soon they left the countryside behind and entered the sprawling city of Genesis. Uriel managed to catch a glimpse of its shining buildings and clean streets, but he didn't get to take in more. As the carriage progressed, his mother pulled him away from the window and lowered the blinds. "You mustn't be seen until tomorrow," she reminded him.

Uriel didn't reply, but she didn't seem to expect it. Outside, a crowd must have already gathered, because cheers rose to greet the carriage. Even through the blinds, Uriel saw the hands reaching out to him as countless people brushed their fingers over the carriage. They didn't rock it—it was forbidden by law, and no one would dare to cause the Guiding Light such discomfort—but they certainly came quite close.

In a way, it was a relief to reach their destination, although when the carriage slowed down and stopped, Uriel had the urge to tell its driver to go back the way they'd come. Of course he didn't do it. Instead, when the carriage door opened, he allowed the force of habit to guide him and stepped outside.

In front of him, the Temple of Genesis rose, a beautiful pyramid that dominated the entire city. Somehow, even if Uriel had lived here once, he always forgot how much it scared him.

But he'd made a decision, and he wouldn't back down. As his so-called parents descended from the carriage and entered the building, Uriel followed them without hesitation. He would be what they wanted him to be—not for himself or for them but for all the people out there who needed him. He simply didn't have any other choice.

BEEP. BEEP. Beep.

The machine steadily marked the heart rhythm of the patient in the cyber tube. Raze watched the face of the man trapped inside, anger and frustration at his own helplessness coursing through him.

Before the virus, his father had been a strong man. After Raze's mother had died in childbirth, he had taken care of Raze and his then-infant brother all by himself. His CC had reached 90 percent, an achievement that few could boast of reaching. It was as far as anyone could go without becoming an actual robot. Absorbing so much cyber tech within his flesh had been a challenge, a fight Raze's father had won—because he had wanted to be the very best in his field, to protect his two beloved sons.

Raze could still remember the night when it had dawned on him that his father was no longer fully human. At age seven, he'd been chasing their household drone, wanting to dismantle it yet again and see what made it tick. They'd burst into the living room, but in the process, the drone had run straight into his father.

It should have hurt him, but instead Raze had watched with awe as the drone collapsed in a heap of twisted metal. His father had grimaced. "Great. Another one we have to replace. When are you going to learn to play with your toys, not with the help?"

Raze had barely heard him, because he could see one of the drone's metal arms still attached to his father's leg. "Father," he said weakly, "your leg."

He'd looked down and released a heavy sigh. "Come on. You probably want to specialize in this in the future anyway."

They'd sat together on the couch, and his father had pressed his thumb to the center of his palm, making his index finger turn into a scalpel. Raze had known all about cyborgs, and he'd realized his father was one, but he'd never witnessed the extent of what implants could do. It was forbidden for children under the age of eight to have any sort of implant—other than their ID chip, of course.

Raze had watched his father disassemble his leg and operate on the wound. It wasn't an easy process to stomach, but he'd grown up with a soldier, so he was used to the sight of blood. However, even as he cut into his own flesh and parted his skin, Raze's father seemed to be monitoring Raze's reactions to the process more than he did the operation.

"It's not a serious wound," he told Raze. "I'll just have to replace one of the transistors."

As Raze watched him do exactly that, he'd wondered what it was like to feel metal where once had been flesh. "Isn't it strange?" he asked his father.

"Strange?" the man had repeated. "Well, some might argue it is. It's a bit of a paradox. I think, Raze, that our body is just a shell. What matters is the soul hiding beneath. My nerve endings might have been replaced with cybernetic circuits, but I'm still your father, and I love you, very, very much. At the same time, my body and my blood—together with that of your mother—gave you life. You have to think carefully before you decide to make such a step. First and foremost, you are a human being. Never lose sight of that."

He had smiled at Raze, and even today, that image still came back to him, together with the knowledge that his father had done all that for Raze and his brother. Ever since that day, his father always cautioned Raze against going too far with implants.

"One day," he had said, "something else will show up, something that will counter all of our technological advancements. It's a law of nature and of balance. No matter how strong you are, there will always be someone who is stronger. So even when you aim for the top, Raze, stay on the cautious side."

He'd been furious with Raze the day his CC had passed fifty, and he'd blamed himself for Raze's decision. He had anticipated Raze would have a lot of problems because of that choice. As it turned out, he'd been completely correct.

Now there his father lay, motionless, only able to remain alive because of the machines Raze so tortuously hid from the purists. It was getting harder and harder to keep their hideout safe from the Genesis priests, because they carefully monitored all energy consumption in the ghettoes. Raze had circumvented that by organizing the resistance in the industrial area of Genesis, but that might not work forever. Basically they—the machine-people, as they were called—were good enough to support the lavish lifestyles of the purists, but they had to be kept powerless, because otherwise, they represented a danger for the perfect Edenian society.

Raze released a heavy sigh as he watched the steady rhythm of the machines. Fixing his gaze on the cyber tube, he willed his mental computer into action. His vision instantly filled with data on his father's condition—starting from his CC to his collapsing lungs and his faltering heart.

Clenching his jaw, Raze finally looked away. This visit cemented his decision. His father was dying. Soon the machines would stop being able to keep him alive. Even if the purists didn't find him, their time was running out.

As Raze turned away from the tube, the door slid open with a whoosh and his brother walked into the room. "How is he?" he mouthed at Raze.

He released no sound, but then he never did. Julian had been born with a beautiful voice, but he'd also been young during the attack of the virus. A lot of the implants had short-circuited, including Julian's ID chip. The process had affected that part of the brain that regulated speech. Now he mostly communicated through sign language, although Raze and many of the other cyborgs understood him by reading his lips. Sometimes Raze didn't even require that. They were brothers, after all.

Sometimes Raze thought it was unfair. To this day, he didn't realize how he hadn't ended up in a cyber tube next to his father. His CC wasn't as high as that of the old soldier, and his vital organs remained as natural as they'd always been, but Raze certainly had enough implants that he should have been a vegetable just the same, or at least a cripple. Instead, Raze had survived without being too much worse for wear. Granted, the only things that remained in functional order were his mental computer and his eye implants, as the other ones had shut down. His speed and strength had decreased, but he could handle that—because for fuck's sake, he was still able to move. All the while, his younger brother had been deprived of his beautiful voice and the ability to communicate.

Raze shook himself and focused on Julian. His brother relied on Raze to be his anchor, and Raze couldn't fail him. "It's bad, Jules," he answered. "He has two weeks left, maybe a month at best."

Julian gritted his teeth, his nostrils flaring. "So you'll be going through with your plan?" he finally signed, now making agitated gestures as well.

"It can't be helped," Raze answered. "It's our last chance if we want to save Father."

"You'll never make it," Julian warned him, "and it could be for naught. You know as well as I do that the Guiding Light is nothing more than an illusion supported by propaganda."

"Yes, I know that. But there have been those who came back from seeing the famous Light claiming an improvement in their respective conditions. It might not be the Light at all, doing that. The purists might have a different method altogether. If that is the case, we need it, for Father's sake."

"But if you go there, the purists will catch sight of you. The resistance can't endure without you as a leader." Julian clutched Raze's shoulders tightly. "Let me go."

Raze shook his head. "It has to be me. My mental computer will allow me to analyze that son of a bitch." He smirked. "Besides, there's no real danger. Their scanners can't detect me since my CC dropped."

Not to mention that they needed evidence regarding the purists' treachery. The cyber resistance, an underground group that Raze led, had been working to achieve this for quite a while now. Showing purist citizens the truth about what happened in the ghettoes would solve nothing. Most knew and didn't care about machine-people anyway.

But if the truth came out about their precious Light…. Well, that was a different matter entirely.

The Guiding Light of Genesis was said to be the one man who was 100 percent flesh. Everyone else had a touch of cyber within them, from people like Raze who'd gained dangerously high CCs before the virus to any regular person with only one or two implants. Even newborn children gained a CC—although it was a very low one. Researchers claimed it had something to do with the aftereffects of previous implants. Pure children couldn't be born from cyborgs, and it would take generations until the gene pool actually started to lose the cyber effect.

All the while, this man, this Light, claimed to have a CC of zero—when he had been born of cyborgs, before the virus, and had actually had a chip implanted. It was impossible, and if Raze got evidence of that, he'd have the entire Edenian political system in the palm of his hand. He would be able to force them into helping his father.

Tomorrow was a ceremonial day, one when the Guiding Light would come to greet the people. The ghettoes would be in complete shutdown. Even the factories stopped working, since the cyborgs were all confined to their respective homes. But those rules didn't always apply for the people who knew how to evade them.

"Don't worry about me," he told Julian. "I'll be fine."

Raze pressed his hand to the scanner next to the door, and it slid open once again. Julian stayed behind, in their father's room. They no longer had drones in working order to assist them with medical care, so an actual person had to be on watch at every hour of the day, lest something happen with the machines keeping Raze's father alive.

Outside, the underground hideout was a rush of activity. Some of the people Raze knew waved at him, but he responded with only a nod. Julian was right about one thing. His plan came with a lot of risks, so he needed to make sure he had someone to back him up.

Raze found his friend Logan in his workshop, tinkering with his VR equipment. He was grumbling under his breath, seemingly attempting to update some of the protocols. As Raze entered the room, Logan greeted him with a grunt. "So, I take it you're going, then?"

"Yeah," Raze replied. "Is everything in place?"

Logan turned to look at him and smirked. "It sure is. You can't imagine what people are willing to do for a free pass at the club."

"Well, we do sell dreams, after all," Raze answered.

Even if Raze was in charge of the security of this place, Logan shouldered the brunt of the administrative tasks. Starting from a comment Raze had once made, he'd developed quite a lucrative business that supplied them with all the funds they needed.

"I hate how the purists act all high and mighty about their untouchable Light," Raze had told him then. "Wouldn't it be funny if it turned out that the man was an absolute pervert?"

Even now, Raze was completely convinced that the so-called law forbidding any sort of contact with the Guiding Light was nothing more than a front to cultivate the mysterious allure of the prophet. Behind closed doors, the false god likely had hundreds of lovers.

His friend had seen potential in Raze's offhand remark. Logan had blinked at him, and then his lips had twisted into a smirk Raze could remember to this day. "You know, you might have something there."

This was how Logan's pet project had come to life—a cyber club where everyone could have whatever sexual pleasures they desired. Most importantly, he had added one important ingredient to the cocktail: the Guiding Light himself.

Courtesy of the way the ceremonial days were held, they had plenty of patrons, even among purists. Of course, no one knew the cyborgs were behind it. The bastards all thought they were perfectly safe, but if Raze revealed their true desires, he could easily ruin more than one purist aristocrat. At the same time, even if all the secrets he had learned through Logan's idea could have come in handy, he couldn't risk the safety of the club yet.

"Just remember not to push things," Raze warned him. "If I get captured…. Make sure you watch over Julian and my father."

Logan immediately sobered. "You don't have to tell me that, Raze. You know you guys are like family to me."

Yes, Raze did know that. And because his family, Logan included, deserved a better life, tomorrow Raze would be leaving the ghetto. He would find out just how much of a god the Guiding Light was.

Chapter Two

THE NEXT day dawned with countless preparations for the ceremony to come. Uriel awoke before the sun's first rays and forced himself to consume a special blend of vitamins with a taste so awful it made his eyes water. He drank it all down regardless, knowing he would need the nutrients. After that, he immediately rushed into the bathing chamber. Mercifully, one benefit of his position was that he could wash himself and in fact needed to do so. Since his body represented the epitome of purity, no one had permission to touch his naked skin. In her official position as Uriel's Guardian, his mother received some allowances, but she was the exception to the rule.

Once clean, Uriel oiled his skin with a special perfumed liquid that he used every ceremonial day. It kept him from sweating and maintained his pristine appearance in spite of his existing physical limitations. Of course it also had certain side effects, since blocking his sweat glands to that extent made him physically ill and the substances in the oil often caused him rashes. But those problems only showed up in the days to come, and he had special remedies to help them pass.

For the moment, it didn't hurt at all, so Uriel could focus on becoming the Guiding Light his people expected him to be. After returning to his room, he combed his hair and found his garments for the day already prepared on the bed. He carefully dressed, paying close attention so he would not tear the delicate fabric.

His outfit consisted of a robe woven manually from silk and gold thread. His mother had made it herself, and after it had been completed, it had gone through a special cleansing process that eliminated all traces of her touch. Uriel never wore the same robe for more than one ceremony, since once they were taken out of the temple they were considered impure.

The robe represented the last barrier Uriel had, the last thing that separated him from what he needed to do today. The knowledge of when it would come off made Uriel taste bile in his mouth. But, as every single time, Uriel hid his dread behind his carefully cultivated mask. As he finished doing the buttons on his robe, he took a deep breath and looked in the mirror.

"Get a hold of yourself, Uriel," he told his reflection. "You're the Guiding Light. You can do this. You have to."

When he thought he'd mustered the right degree of composure, Uriel left the room. Unlike the day before, he didn't bind his hair back. It trailed behind him, brushing over the pristine floor of the Temple of Genesis in a long curtain of blond locks. Uriel actually liked leaving his hair loose, but only when he was alone and didn't risk anyone touching him. Therefore, today would be next to nightmarish for his sensibilities.

Uriel walked alone through the corridors of the temple. Apprentices and monks knelt in front of him, letting him pass without a word. At last, he reached the exit of the temple. His mother and Councilman Ezekiel were waiting for him there.

"Excellent," Ezekiel said, eyeing Uriel from head to toe. "Now, we have quite a turnout today, so make sure you are patient and kind to everyone."

For some reason, that phrase flipped a switch in Uriel's mind. He'd accepted the responsibility he'd been given, but since he had done so, he wanted the Council to acknowledge him as was his due.

25

"I appreciate the advice, Councilman Ezekiel," he answered, "but I am the Guiding Light. I am *always* patient and kind."

Perhaps the words came out more sarcastic than was appropriate, but Uriel didn't appreciate their looking down on him when his mother had made it so clear to him that this was his role and his burden to carry. He was tired of being treated like a child when he'd already reached twenty years of age. Not to mention that Uriel had never failed them before. As much as he complained in private, he had never let the weak part of him show.

Ezekiel clenched his jaw but smiled tightly. "Of course. I realize that, Your Holiness. I didn't mean to offend."

"Oh, you didn't offend me," Uriel told the other man. "I just meant to reassure you that everything will be all right. In the end, I'm your Guiding Light too. Isn't that right, Head Councilman?"

"Indeed, and I consider myself lucky to live in such blessed times," Ezekiel replied.

"As do I," Uriel's mother piped up.

Uriel wondered if they really believed that. Perhaps they did, if only because of the privileged position they'd received due to their blood relation with him. But Uriel had lingered here for too long already. He couldn't delay the ceremony. His people were waiting.

"Guardian Abigail, Councilman Ezekiel, thank you for all your assistance," he told them formally. "I promise I won't fail you."

With that, he pushed out of the temple inner cloister and stepped outside. The temple was erected in the shape of a pyramid, so that when he walked out, he found himself on a large platform that opened into a huge agora. Black-clad guards stood by on the platform, like quiet monoliths entrusted with the task of keeping Uriel safe.

Uriel's breath caught as he took in the number of people that filled the agora. Councilman Ezekiel hadn't been joking when he'd said there had been a good turnout. In fact, that might have been an understatement. There was no way Uriel could see so many believers in one single day.

In that moment, as Uriel stood in front of the thousands of people who had gathered to see him, he felt the weight of the world on his shoulders. How could he deny the obvious when faced with such an overwhelming truth? All of these men and women would have probably been horrified if they'd seen him yesterday, craving the small pleasure of a romance novel.

Uriel did his best to calm down and walked to the edge of the platform. "Greetings," he called out. "I thank you for coming to see me this day. Approach, my children, and let me hear your woes. I am here for you. I am your Guiding Light."

They were the traditional words Uriel always spoke on ceremonial days, but the crowd cheered anyway. Even so, no one moved. They all knew to wait for the actual beginning of the process.

Taking a deep breath, Uriel reached for the buttons of his robe and undid them. The garment slid to the ground, leaving him standing naked in front of the entire audience. Ceremonial days had become harder as Uriel grew into an adult, and he still wasn't fully used to being completely nude. Things had been so much easier during his childhood years. At the very least, back then, the Council hadn't forced him into exposing his privates.

The crowd grew silent, but Uriel had to stare into the horizon to gather his bearings. He distantly wondered what had happened to Scott and Eric. Had they been happy in the end? Undoubtedly. They'd been very much in love—at least, according to the story. What was it like to feel love? Uriel didn't know, and he would probably never find out, not when his life rotated around such events.

Shaking himself, Uriel directed his attention toward the crowd of believers. They were the only ones he would ever be allowed to show affection toward, even if it was a shallow, crippled thing. But it wasn't their fault for not realizing it. They were only seeking their beacon, their Guiding Light. Who was Uriel to refuse them the happiness he'd been denied?

As the first believer approached, Uriel smiled at him and said, "May you be blessed this day. What ails you, my child?"

27

The man stared at Uriel with such awe he felt guilty for his own doubts and fears. "I…. My implant… it's been giving me migraines."

Uriel brought his fingers close to the man's forehead without actually touching him. If he wanted to be perfectly honest, he'd always been able to sense the implants in people. It wasn't something he could put his finger on, but he saw the technology in many of the men and women who came to visit him. Half the time, these citizens lived with the burden of implants that couldn't be removed because of the extreme way they had bonded with their host body. More often than not, the plagued area was the brain—a particularly sensitive zone in the human body.

But even if Uriel could feel the implants, he highly doubted he could do anything about them. He was no doctor, and he had moments when he felt like the only assistance he gave these people was nothing more than a form of placebo. Nevertheless, Uriel closed his eyes and wished he really did have the power to soothe this man's aches.

All of a sudden, the believer in front of him gasped. Uriel opened his eyes, only to see the man staggering back, his body shuddering as if in rapture. "Thank you," he murmured in awe and maybe just a little lust. Gripping Uriel's hair, he kissed the long blond locks. "Thank you, Your Holiness."

The man cast a glance over Uriel's shoulder, where Uriel knew a guard was hovering. At last, with a heavy sigh, he pulled back, making no move to touch Uriel anywhere else. Soon he'd disappeared into the crowd, and another petitioner had taken his place, this time a female.

The story repeated itself more than once. It was unfortunate, but it couldn't be helped. The believers were not allowed to show sexual desire toward the Guiding Light since Uriel was considered beyond such things. Nonetheless, it stood to reason that, since Uriel appeared in front of them naked, very palpable and within their reach, there would be some lust involved.

As long as the people in question didn't act on it, the guards wouldn't remove them. Even so, for Uriel it all remained taxing and unpleasant. He wanted to believe this was a religious process and his role as a Guiding Light important, but given the circumstances, he felt sullied and violated. More than once, Uriel had asked his mother to allow him a garment that would cover his genitals. It had been allowed before he'd come of age, in deference to his youth. Now his request had been denied on the basis that his body belonged to the people, and they were supposed to see his purity.

Yet again, Uriel could find no way out. He didn't have the right to feel lust—he actually had to consume a libido suppressor before stepping out onto the platform—but he had to face it in such blatant displays. Perhaps he simply felt jealous of such a simple thing, that they could experience desire when he was denied that. In any case, the way their eyes lingered on him was one of the reasons Uriel hated ceremonial days so much.

Still, he could not refuse the people the solution to their problems. Whether he could truly heal them or not, they obviously believed it to be so. And so he went on with the ceremony, clinging to his own smiling mask like an anchor.

THE CROWD in front of the Temple of Genesis probably amounted to thousands of people, all of them standing in line to greet their god and prophet, the Guiding Light. Young and old, they waited for their turn to come for hours on end. If children cried, their mothers silenced them. "This is important," a woman said to her son. "You have to meet the Guiding Light so that one day you'll grow as strong as he is."

Someone else scoffed behind her. "Don't lie to the boy. No one can ever be like our Guiding Light."

The woman's face flamed as the rest of the so-called believers gathered around her, nudging her and sneering. "I didn't mean it that way," she said, holding her son close. "I was only trying to soothe him."

No one paid any heed to her words, and Raze couldn't bear the sight of such a scene. Taking a step forward, he said, "Stop. Do you really think the Guiding Light would want you to act this way?"

The men and women around them shared uncomfortable looks but backed off. Raze could only wonder for the millionth time that day if he might have made a mistake in coming here. So far, the entire affair only disgusted him. He had yet to spot the Guiding Light, even though he'd been here in the early hours of the morning. While he could be very patient when he needed to, he couldn't help but wonder if he was taking a foolish chance.

Hundreds of mounted guards supervised the area, carrying old-fashioned-looking pistols. Raze knew the only thing ancient about them was their appearance, because actually they were phasers equipped with the latest technology in detecting cybernetic coefficient. If one cyborg with a CC past 50 percent entered the area, those phasers would detect them. After all, the machine-people couldn't touch the precious, perfect Guiding Light.

Raze's CC was 80 percent, or it had been, before the virus. Now after his implants had deactivated, it hovered at 49 percent, just below the detectable limit. Technically speaking, he still shouldn't have been here—legally, only citizens with a 20 percent CC or below were allowed to such ceremonies—but fortunately, the discrepancy between the law and the equipment enforcing it allowed him this visit. In any case, Raze had taken precautions to ensure his escape should a problem appear, and the fact remained that this was possibly the last thing that could save his father. Otherwise, he would have never chanced showing up in front of the Guiding Light, especially not today.

It was almost funny to think that, with all of their preaching of purity, the purists had created a ceremony that included their god taking his clothes off. Raze had seen images of it—who hadn't, after all?—and he couldn't imagine how anyone would consider that sort of thing a purely religious experience. The Guiding Light was a very beautiful, sensual man, one whom Raze would have....

Raze frowned, squashing the thought before it could fully form. He could be as appreciative of the Guiding Light's looks as any other guy, but this wasn't about that. That man represented everything that was so very wrong in this world, all of the persecution cyborgs had been going through since the virus. There were factions in the ghetto who wanted to kill him, and Raze himself might have done it if he hadn't realized all too well that such a thing would only make matters worse. Turning the Guiding Light into a martyr would guarantee a purist counterattack that would deliver the final blow to Raze's people. Besides, this man was just the face of a far more complex regime. The Council, a group of corrupt aristocrats, backed his every move.

Well, today would largely be a scouting mission that would reveal the CC of the Guiding Light. Since Raze could detect most of the tech in the area, he'd also be able to note what kind of methods the purists used to help the people. In the end, the Guiding Light himself didn't matter, but what he could give Raze.

As Raze mused over this, the line finally started to advance. At last Raze entered the agora and caught a glimpse of what he'd been waiting for.

A young man stood on the platform erected in front of the temple. He was surrounded by guards, and a stream of believers constantly moved toward him, and yet he seemed to shine, his light overwhelming everything around him.

Was it a hallucination or some sort of trick from the purists? Raze forced himself to think that, because there was simply no other explanation. Frowning, he zoomed in to the young man using his eye implants. Raze was still so far away from him, but it didn't matter. Even from this distance, his improved senses could take in the Guiding Light as he stood there, literally in the flesh.

Raze had known Guiding Light Uriel Noah of the House of Zion would be beautiful. Many times, he'd used that beauty for the benefit of Logan's club. Nothing had prepared him for this, for his first glimpse of the man behind the propaganda.

His blonde hair flowed all the way to the ground in a wave of gold, and every time a believer approached, they touched the Guiding Light's locks. His beautiful body was exposed for all to see, and even if no one dared to make contact with his skin, it still filled Raze with anger and frustration. Because when Raze looked at the Guiding Light's eyes—his lovely green eyes—Raze saw something there, an emotion he hadn't expected to find in a man in his position. Loneliness, so much loneliness.

For the first time, it registered for Raze exactly how a young man his age would feel when faced with doing something like this. It would be a humiliation and a violation of privacy at the very least. But why did that matter to Raze? However lonely and embarrassed the Guiding Light might feel, he remained Raze's enemy. Raze needed to find out exactly what made him tick, especially now. The Guiding Light was notorious for holding long ceremonial days, during which he never stopped giving his blessings—not even to eat, rest, or go to the bathroom. Yes, there had to be some sort of implant involved.

As Raze continued to look at the Guiding Light, his mental computer processed the data it had already been fed. CC 0 percent, it reported. Raze barely managed to suppress a gasp. It couldn't be. Exactly what was going on here, and how had the purists managed to eliminate their leader's CC?

More importantly, if he truly had no implants, he couldn't do anything to help these people—which meant he couldn't help Raze's father either. And yet, even from the distance, Raze saw the tears of relief on the faces of those who managed to reach him. Using the filters in his eye implants, Raze scanned the area of the platform for any sort of tech that could be helping the Guiding Light. While he could easily detect the weaponry the temple guards used, there didn't seem to be any sort of cybernetic equipment around the Guiding Light at all.

Clearly, Raze wouldn't get an answer until he finally reached the Guiding Light. Therefore he settled himself in for a long wait. His attention turned to the Light's naked body. He couldn't help but wonder how it would feel to touch him. It was just curiosity of course, and his normal need for information. After all, if Raze knew that sort of thing, he could improve on Logan's VR engine.

Even as Raze tried to convince himself of this, his eyes met those of the Guiding Light. A strange sort of awareness seemed to pass through the young man's green orbs. Impossibly, he was looking straight at Raze, but that couldn't be right. A noncyborg couldn't possibly see Raze in the gathered crowd—not to mention that Raze had paid special attention to not standing out.

And still, even as he advanced through the agora, Raze felt the other man's eyes on him. His heart started hammering, and he wondered if all the people here experienced this powerful pull toward their leader. It was almost like a gravitational attraction. With every second that passed, he realized more and more that he shouldn't have come here, that he'd underestimated the Guiding Light and possibly the purists as a whole. But it was too late to back down. His very being rebelled against the thought of turning tail and running.

It seemed to take forever until Raze reached the edge of the platform. In front of him, the woman with the boy brought her son to face the Guiding Light. Raze had to admit that having a naked man facing a young child was terribly inappropriate. From Raze's angle, he could easily tell the Guiding Light was uncomfortable with the situation, but he made no move to pick up his fallen robe. He did, however, flip his hair just so, using the heavy mass to cover most of his front side. Raze thought the move was quite clever.

No sooner had the Guiding Light completed his little scheme than the boy's mother bowed in front of her supposed prophet. "I would ask for your blessing for my child," she whispered.

"You are already blessed," the Guiding Light replied. "A young life is the purest form of benediction that can possibly exist." He smiled at her and lowered one of his hands over both the child and the woman, while using the other to hold his hair in place. "But you are always in my prayers as well. May you be blessed this day and from today henceforth, for as long as Genesis itself stands and into the future."

The woman gasped, while the child stared in rapt awe at the figure in front of him. For a few moments, Raze thought he saw something flash between the three, but that instant passed before he could get a good glimpse of what the odd thing had been.

At last the woman and the child bowed lowly. They brushed their fingers over the locks of hair that fell within their reach and away from the Guiding Light's body. They pulled away, and it was finally Raze's turn to approach his target. Someone on the platform cleared his throat, and the Guiding Light released his hold on his hair, fully exposing himself again.

Even as he walked to the Guiding Light's side, Raze said nothing. His vocal cords seemed frozen, and his body had gone on autopilot. He should have felt humiliated for kneeling in front of this man, but he did so without a second of hesitation.

The Guiding Light didn't speak either. His breath caught, and he faltered, almost like he wanted to step back. Raze's mental computer registered a change in his heart rate and the heat his body let out. But before the reasons for that could truly process, he took a deep breath and brushed his fingers over Raze's forehead.

He didn't actually touch Raze, but it didn't matter. Stars exploded in Raze's vision. Suddenly he couldn't breathe, and his mind started to whirl with a million ideas he couldn't process. "System shutdown imminent," his mental computer warned him. "System shutdown imminent."

What the fuck? Was he going to die like this, with his brain short-circuited by a man too beautiful for words? It was almost laughable. The virus hadn't managed to kill him and fully destroy his implants, but this, this mysterious person had succeeded where that horrible plague had failed.

Raze's human brain attempted to recover from the shock, but it had been far too powerful. He didn't know how much time passed until finally Raze's mental computer started up again. "System reboot."

The world became clear again, and as Raze opened his eyes, he found himself lying on a low settee with the Guiding Light looming over him. He was even more beautiful up close, and before Raze could think about his own actions, he reached for the young man. The Guiding Light released a gasp and moved away before Raze could touch him.

For a few moments, the two of them just looked at each other. Raze was uncertain as to what exactly had happened, and even that would have been enough to make his hackles rise. It certainly didn't help that his senses were on overload. He could distinguish every perfect pore of the Guiding Light's face, scent his light, clean perfume. It was getting to Raze's head as much as his light touch had.

Forcing himself to shut down those feelings, Raze focused on his current environment. He'd obviously been taken out of the agora, into an unfamiliar-looking room. He needed to get out of there as soon as possible, because otherwise, not even his brilliant contingency plans would be able to help him. "What happened?" Raze asked. "Where am I?"

"You collapsed in front of me," the Guiding Light replied, his voice soft as he eyed Raze from head to toe. At some point, he'd bound his hair back, and he wasn't naked any longer, instead wearing an elaborately embroidered robe. "I asked the guards to carry you here. You're in a room in the Temple of Genesis. But... you must go quickly. I don't know if I can stop them once they find out who you really are."

All of the muscles in Raze's body seized and froze. He met the other man's gaze, remembering that brief moment when his hand had hovered over Raze's forehead, when he'd felt the strange jolt of energy course through his body. Could it be? Had he been the one to cause that? How?

The only explanation Raze could come up with was the Guiding Light had some sort of bioenergy, perhaps as a remnant of his surviving the virus. That made sense, although if that was so, Raze couldn't fathom why the Guiding Light's CC hadn't been affected by all the times he'd come into contact with cyborgs.

Either way, he obviously knew about Raze's true identity—or at the very least, that his CC disqualified him from being here. Confirming Raze's thoughts, the Guiding Light added, "I kept them out after your implants started working again, but it will be strange if I linger here for much longer. You must leave as soon as possible."

At the very least, he didn't seem to plan to hand Raze over to the purists—a positive in Raze's book. Nonetheless, that didn't mean no risks existed with regard to Raze's capture. He should have taken the Guiding Light's suggestion, but if he left now, he'd never get a chance like this again. He needed to find out if this strange, beautiful man could help his father.

As he got up, Raze accessed his mental computer and found it in perfect working order. He couldn't pull up the plans of the Temple of Genesis, at least not without a physical local area connection. Still, given that all of his implants had miraculously recovered, he'd probably be able to bypass temple security without too much trouble.

Maybe he would have chanced it and proceeded with a daring escape similar to the ones from the ancient movies his father had once watched with him. But if there was one thing he'd learned from those nigh-embarrassingly unrealistic shows, it had to be that the one-man-army thing didn't work when the so-called hero had someone else tagging along.

And speaking of which, Raze needed to address this little matter with the Guiding Light. "You're coming with me," he said, grabbing the Guiding Light's arm.

The young man's eyes widened. "What? No, I can't...."

"You can," Raze answered. "Do you truly want to stay with these people? Don't think I didn't notice how the entire ceremony made you feel. Hurt, angry, alone, humiliated. Like a piece of meat."

Even as he spoke, Raze realized he was being cruel, twisting the knife in a still-bleeding wound. Indeed, electricity crackled between them as the Guiding Light tried to move away. Raze hadn't touched the younger man's flesh, but he still felt it, all throughout his body. Oddly enough, it made his cock throb painfully.

The Guiding Light seemed unaware of his effect on Raze. "You cannot possibly understand. This is my duty. These days are set aside for religious gatherings. What would those people out there do if I left?"

Raze didn't bother to point out that, in his opinion, few people in the crowd had any religious thoughts. He himself admitted to being guilty of that. But telling the Guiding Light such a thing would make things worse, especially since Raze suspected the young man already knew.

"Fair enough," Raze said in the end. "But have you ever wondered about those people who cannot approach you? People like me who suffer in silence because your poisonous regime just isolates us. We're good enough to serve as tools in your factories, but we are forbidden from even being in the presence of their precious Guiding Light."

At that, the young man faltered. "Sometimes I do wonder. But... I don't know anything of what happens beyond the walls of the temple and my residence. I'm told that there is a resistance which means to target my life, but I gather that if you'd been part of it, I'd already be dead."

Raze stared at him, meeting the guileless green eyes of the man the purists considered their god and prophet. He was just as trapped in the world the upper echelons had created. Raze had always considered him a symbol of everything that was wrong with their society, but he could now see so very clearly that he was a person like any other—and a naïve one at that.

A part of Raze wanted to point out he was the leader of that same resistance, but telling the truth would just make the young man wary of him. Instead, he said, "I came here because my father is very sick. He has a very high CC, and his entire body nearly shut down

37

when the virus struck. I didn't believe that you could make someone's implants work again or help them in any way. But now that I've seen it with my own eyes…. You can help him. Save his life."

The Guiding Light hesitated. "I…. Everyone here… I don't know what to do."

Raze made a split-second decision. If he made a mistake here, he could fuck things up beyond measure. But no matter how many mechanical parts he might have, his heart and his soul remained those of a human—and they spoke to him, telling him it was time to have faith.

It wouldn't be blind, religious faith in the Guiding Light, but a trust in the decency of the young man who could have given him up but hadn't.

Taking a deep breath, Raze reached for the Guiding Light's— no, Uriel's—hands. "Listen… Uriel. I'm going to be fully honest with you. My name is Raze Hartman, and I am part of the resistance. We never aimed to kill you, although I have to admit that at one time we did consider it. I see now that we were wrong. Help me. Please."

Chapter Three

URIEL STOOD there, frozen, as he took in the touch of the stranger's—no, Raze's—warm hands. It was explicitly forbidden—people were only ever allowed to touch his hair. His mother was partially exempt from that rule, but for anyone else, touching the Guiding Light remained punishable by law.

He didn't know what to think or what to feel. The cyborg had confessed to plotting his murder—sort of. But at the same time, he felt so warm, nothing like the way his mother had described the "machine-people." Raze's deep, dark eyes scrutinized Uriel with an intensity that should have scared him but instead made a strange yearning stir inside him.

No one had ever looked at him like he was more than a thing, like he was a person who could decide for himself what he wanted to do. This man, a member of the fabled resistance, was giving Uriel a choice. Yes, he'd forced Uriel to face the uncomfortable truth he'd been trying to hide from, but he'd also shown him a glimpse of a reality that he had not known. And he'd called Uriel by his name.

Even as his mind whirled with confusion and uncertainty, his body heated at the unfamiliar touch. Electricity coursed through him at the simple hold, making him hyperaware of every nerve ending in his body. Not even the libido suppressor he'd consumed could stand its ground when faced with Raze's presence. Uriel's face flamed, and he quickly removed his hands from the stranger's grasp. Raze blinked, as if not understanding his attitude, and then realization seemed to dawn. His full lips twisted in a sarcastic smirk.

"Oh, I see. The machine-man isn't good enough to touch the Guiding Light. My apologies, Your Holiness. It seems I was mistaken to believe—"

"Stop!" Uriel blurted out, breathing hard, wishing he hadn't bound his hair back so he could hide behind it. "Don't say that. Just stop."

Raze did stop. For a few moments, he stared at Uriel like he'd never seen him before. "It's true, isn't it? What the purists say. You truly don't touch anyone."

Uriel nodded jerkily, then explained. "It's true. My mother is the only exception."

As he looked at Raze, Uriel wondered if his new acquaintance had felt that bolt of electricity too. If so, he didn't show it. Uriel didn't know whether to feel relieved or disappointed. He chose relief—because the last thing he needed right now was for this man to realize how much Uriel craved the simplest form of affection.

In the end, his own confused emotions didn't matter. If this man was telling the truth, there could be other people who needed his help. It shamed Uriel that he'd never considered cyborgs more than tentative enemies. Now he knew better, and he had to make it up to Raze and his people.

"I will help you, but it can't be now," he said. "I've already stayed here too long. The Council will come fetch me, and if they don't find me, they'll alert the guards. We'd never get away."

He couldn't believe what he was saying to a virtual stranger. Even so, he had understood long ago that allowing himself to be caught up in the pace of the Council made him feel empty inside. Maybe he'd realized all along that there might be other things for him out there, his true purpose in life. And maybe he was being rash by accepting Raze's words at face value, but in his heart, he felt like he could trust the other man.

Raze hummed thoughtfully at his comment. "Perhaps you're right. If you leave now, your believers will mob."

Uriel hadn't actually meant it that way, although he had worried about what his departure might mean for the people who needed his help. The realization settled into renewed determination, and all of a sudden, he knew exactly what he needed to do.

The cyborg seemed to guess that, because he arched a brow. "You have an idea. What are you thinking?"

Uriel licked his lips nervously. "You need to…. Just…. You have a mental computer, right?"

"Yes, but you knew that already," Raze replied. "What's the plan?"

"The ceremonies will probably last two days," Uriel explained. "After that, I'll need at least one day to recover. By that time, the Council will lose interest in me and they'll leave me alone. You can come pick me up at the compound where I live, in four days. Is that fast enough? How serious is your father's condition?"

"He's dying," Raze replied bluntly, "but I understand the necessity of the wait. Four days should be fine. I take it you want to show me my target through my mental computer?"

Uriel hesitated. "I've never tried this before," he warned the cyborg. "Until now, I didn't actually think I had much power at all. This might not work."

Even so, he needed to make the attempt. If he couldn't do this, it was highly unlikely that he could even help Raze's father. As if guessing Uriel's thoughts, Raze nodded and closed his eyes. "Go ahead, Uriel. I trust you."

Somehow those simple words gave Uriel strength. The faith of others had always been a burden for him, but with Raze, it seemed different. Against all odds, this so-called machine-man had taken his chances with trusting someone he must have hated for the better part of his life. It wasn't the Guiding Light Raze saw but Uriel, as he was, with his flaws, his fears and uncertainties.

Taking a deep breath, Uriel approached Raze. For a few moments, he just stood there, trembling slightly, his fingers hovering over Raze's face as he struggled to process every thought and emotion. Given that Raze had closed his eyes, Uriel could unashamedly admire the other man's masculine face. The sharp angles of his cheekbones and his aquiline nose gave the impression of harshness, but his full lips and the apparent softness of his closely cropped hair toned it down. Uriel wondered if, given the chance, Raze would want to kiss him like Scott had done to Eric.

Uriel quickly shook away the thoughts and pressed his hand to Raze's cheek. The contact was, literally, electric. Uriel's breath caught, and he reeled back, his body overwhelmed by unfamiliar sensations. He might have run out of the room, but Raze wrapped an arm around him and pulled him close.

As Raze held him flush against his hard body, Uriel went rigid. His dislike at being forced into something returned with a vengeance. But then he noticed that Raze made no attempt to touch his skin. He embraced Uriel tightly, keeping his hands on Uriel's waist, where his garments blocked any possibility of actual contact.

Raze's warmth and his masculine scent fascinated Uriel. "It's all right," Raze whispered. "I won't hurt you. I won't ever hurt you. I promise that."

The cyborg's voice flowed over Uriel like a physical caress—one he could accept without question. And Uriel believed him with every fiber of his being. Closing his eyes too, he tried again.

This time when the jolt came, Uriel didn't shy away from it. He embraced it, prodding at the power that had been lying dormant up until this point. Somewhere within him, doors of self-restraint burst open, and Uriel leaned against Raze's chest as their minds connected. Brief flashes of memory pierced Uriel's mind, images he couldn't make sense of. He saw snapshots of people he didn't know and caught garbled pieces of conversation.

"It's bad, Jules. I don't think he'll make it until next week."

"If I get captured…. Make sure you watch over Julian and my father."

"Stop. Do you really think the Guiding Light would want you to act this way?"

"System shutdown imminent."

At last Uriel managed to pinpoint the part of Raze's mind that connected with an implanted computer. The world cleared, the hectic sway of human emotion settling down into the shockingly comforting hum of the machine. Looking around with eyes that went beyond the physical, Uriel became fascinated by the way brain synapses connected with microchips. He'd been taught that the blend between man and machine created monsters, but Uriel saw harmony—one different from pure nature but beautiful nevertheless. He saw that, at the end of the day, cyborgs were just as human as any of them, and he wanted to help this particular cyborg more than ever.

Knowing he didn't have a lot of time, Uriel brought up his memories of the compound and fed them into Raze's mental computer. His recollections were hardly a reliable map, but Uriel had faith that the analytic power of the implant would manage to put them together into a coherent image of the area. He stopped as he allowed Raze's mental computer to process the information, then repeated the influx with what little knowledge he had of the current Temple of Genesis. Raze would need it to escape.

At last he pulled back, opening his eyes and breaking out of Raze's embrace with no small amount of reluctance. Straightening his robes, he struggled to catch his breath and gain control of his body. Raze's proximity had an unexpected and somewhat embarrassing effect on him. While he was fairly certain he'd felt Raze's erection against his hip, he couldn't pursue any potential physical attraction between them.

"Did it work?" he asked, surprised when his voice came out only a little shaky.

Raze opened his eyes and stared at him with an expression Uriel couldn't interpret. "Yes," he finally replied. "I have what I need. And don't worry. I'll get you out of there."

The cyborg's jaw clenched, and his gaze showed a steely determination that hadn't been there before. Uriel didn't know what to make of it. He hoped he hadn't somehow hurt Raze by flooding him with the information.

Uriel wanted to ask, but the sound of approaching footsteps kept him from doing so. "You have to go, now," he told Raze. "My mother is coming."

He'd had great trouble convincing her to leave him alone with Raze in the first place. He'd insisted that the Council members needed to be outside to pacify the crowd, which had become agitated when Raze had fainted. He'd assured her that nothing could possibly go wrong when they were in the temple, with so many guards around. Most importantly, he'd pointed out that the faith of one believer could shake that of many others, and to prevent such a situation, it was essential that Uriel attend to the fallen man. That had been the chief argument that had softened her up—coupled with Uriel's promise that he would stay for two days of ceremony if need be.

She must have gotten tired of waiting, because any moment now she would burst in. Biting his lip, Uriel cursed himself for dwelling so long on the conversation. She was too close now, far too close for Raze to make a clean escape.

"Breathe, Uriel," Raze told him. "I'll be fine."

With a smile thrown Uriel's way, Raze took a few steps back, then ran straight toward the wall—and up it. He caught hold of the wooden beam that supported the ceiling and crawled between it and the large ornament that depicted the symbol of the Temple of Genesis. Uriel couldn't even tell he was there—and he knew where to look.

When his mother walked into the room, Uriel pretended to be busy combing his hair. She frowned at him and looked around the room, sniffing the air like she expected to detect Raze by scent. "Where's the fallen believer?"

"I showed him out," Uriel replied, pulling up the mask that always helped him during ceremonial days.

His mother's scowl deepened as she pinned him with a glacial look. "Truly? When?"

"A few minutes ago," Uriel answered. "He seemed a little shaken but otherwise grateful."

"I'm not comfortable with some stranger running around the Temple of Genesis unattended." She sighed heavily. "I should have known better than to leave you here alone with him."

She waved the guards who always flanked her to approach. "Find the believer. Make sure he leaves the premises safely."

"Yes, Guardian Abigail," the guards said as one.

Uriel didn't address her command, because he knew that would make her more suspicious. Instead, he set aside his brush and wrapped himself tighter in his robes. Just like he'd known would happen, the motion drew her attention to him. "Well then, what are you waiting for?" she asked with a dissatisfied huff. "The people need you."

Uriel forced a meaningless smile to his lips and hoped his panic didn't show. "I know, Guardian Abigail. I'm ready."

RAZE WAITED until Uriel and the woman—his mother—left the room and then dropped to the floor. Everything inside him rebelled against abandoning Uriel here, but as much as he hated it, he knew Uriel was right. Raze couldn't just kidnap him and hope for the best. They had to do this right if they hoped to have any chance of success.

Carefully, Raze slipped out of the room, scanning the corridor with his newly improved senses. Courtesy of Uriel's memories, he had an idea of his current location and how to get out. Running into guards would be a problem, since their devices would now detect his over-the-top CC, and the temple had sensors all over the place that did the same thing. Also, if the surveillance system didn't detect him walking out of the temple, Uriel's word would be suspect, and that could cause complications they couldn't afford. Similarly, if the cameras in the hallways spotted him, Uriel's mother could check the timeline and realize he'd been in the room when she'd come to get her son—which would, again, be problematic.

Thankfully, Raze's now-working implants provided him with the perfect solution. He found the first camera and scanned it quickly, finding its blind spot with ease. It was a single moment during which the device missed one particular area, nearly undetectable with the naked eye. Raze used it to his advantage and sneaked past it. Just like in the room, he used his momentum to scale the wall, supporting himself against the beam. Once above the camera, he used his wrist implant—an improved optic version of the age-old screwdriver—to gain access to its circuits.

All of the computer systems in the Temple of Genesis were linked to one loop. The files were obscenely well guarded and would have required a lot of time to hack into, time Raze didn't have. Even so, he did manage to send a shutdown code that took out all of the equipment in the building. Raze couldn't reach the weapons of the guards—those were individually powered—so he'd have to use his cunning to get rid of that obstacle.

When he was certain the cameras were out of the way, he dropped onto the floor once more. Steeling himself for what would most likely be a difficult confrontation, he headed toward the side exit he'd seen in Uriel's mind.

Just as he'd predicted, he soon ran into the guards Guardian Abigail had sent after him. Pretending to be a little dizzy, he swayed and leaned against the wall. The men came his way, and one of them asked, "Hey, are you okay?"

Raze sighed dreamily. "I don't think I've ever been better. The Guiding Light is… I'm so…. Overwhelmed."

He felt nauseated at having to pretend he was one of the brainwashed believers, but at the same time, a part of him really *was* overwhelmed—by the realization of how wrong he'd been about Uriel. Thankfully, that must have convinced the guards, because they supported him without bothering to retrieve their sensor-equipped guns. "We can understand that," one of them said indulgently.

"You are so lucky to be able to serve him," Raze commented. "I'm so lucky to be able to live in this blessed time when he graces the world with his presence."

He kept chatting with the two guards, who seemed to wholeheartedly agree with any praise or reverential comment directed at Uriel. Then again, their worshipfulness of Uriel likely explained why they hadn't bothered to check Raze over with their scanners. After all, their Guiding Light could do no wrong. He'd have been able to tell if Raze was a dangerous intruder from the first touch. Ironically, they were right, and if not for Uriel's kindness, Raze might have been in a huge predicament right about now.

The guards saw Raze to the door without seeming suspicious of him at all. Once they led him out, Raze was instantly engulfed by the curious, restless crowd. A million questions were thrown his way.

"Did you go inside the temple?"

"Were you able to touch the Guiding Light?"

"How did it feel to be so close to His Holiness?"

Raze gave them all the same meaningless responses he'd prepared for the guards. They would have likely swarmed him like ants, but they lost interest when Uriel emerged on the platform again.

As he watched the young man drop his robe for the second time that day, Raze dug his fingernails into his palms. His mental computer might have processed Uriel's memories into coherent maps—but his heart had interpreted them in an entirely different way.

Uriel was as much of a prisoner of this poisonous system as Raze and his family. He needed someone to save him from his gilded cage, someone to love him like he deserved.

As the thought processed in Raze's mind, he quickly forced himself to push it away. Raze couldn't be the man to provide Uriel the affection he needed, but he could help rescue him from the people who called themselves his protectors. And because he knew that, Raze turned away from Uriel and left the agora. He had an expedition to plan.

WHEN URIEL stepped out onto the platform for the second time that day, wild cheers rose all around him. It shouldn't have surprised Uriel, and in a way it didn't, but it did make him hesitate. His mother shot him a look, and on cue, Uriel dropped his robe and stepped forward, ready to resume the torturous process.

"Come to me, my children," he called out just like he'd always been taught. "I can give you solace."

Even as he spoke, his gaze scanned the crowd, seeking one particular figure. It might have been a stupid thing to do. In the sea of men and women, he couldn't hope to pinpoint Raze.

And yet, impossibly, Raze drew him like some sort of magnet, because Uriel managed to catch a glimpse of him. In truth, that might have had more to do with the fact that Raze was the only man moving away from the pyramid instead of approaching it, but whatever the reason, it made Uriel happy.

For a few seconds, he allowed himself the luxury of watching the other man make his way to safety. He'd been so afraid his mother would figure out the truth about Raze, but now.... Now he could continue with the ceremonial day, no matter how torturous it might be.

When the next believer approached him, Uriel found himself clinging to that image, to Raze's promise and the feel of Raze's body against him. Much to his dismay, his dick twitched, and Uriel was reminded of the problem he'd first encountered when he'd been in the same room with Raze.

He tried to control it and focused on his environment instead. Predictably, his body lost interest, but it was too late. His mother must have noticed the brief episode. Two guards blocked the crowd's sight of him while she offered him a vial of the libido suppressor.

"Here," she said. "Drink this."

As much as he hated it, Uriel quickly downed the substance. Nausea roiled through him as the liquid attacked his body. His blood boiled in his veins. His skin itched, and harsh, ruthless pain pooled into his dick. Uriel temporarily leaned against his mother, clutching his privates and wanting nothing more than to curl into a ball and sleep.

"Stop being so dramatic," his mother said, pushing him away with barely concealed disgust. "I told you once before: it's your own lusts that are your downfall."

She spoke softly, so much so that Uriel barely heard her at all. Uriel took advantage of that and didn't acknowledge her words. It was better to accept the situation and leave it at that, because at this rate, she'd come up with some other method that would castrate him for good. She probably hadn't done so already only because it would mean messing with his perfection. In any case, Uriel didn't want to taunt her with his weaknesses.

Straightening his back, Uriel stepped around the guards and allowed the process to continue. He blessed people and summoned his energy to help their implants. He wondered how he'd missed that power before, because it seemed so obvious now, and it came to him so naturally. And seeing the tears of gratitude on their faces was worth the price he had to pay to be close to them.

Or... it would have been worth it if, at one point, several men hadn't started to shove each other in an attempt to get closer to him. They trampled others with no regard for who could get hurt. His mother didn't even have time to remove him from the platform. The miniature riot was quickly contained and the injured carried away, the process continuing without a hitch in spite of the blood now staining the ground in the agora.

Uriel would have cried, and not out of gratitude. But he killed his tears before they could form because they wouldn't help. And this time when he summoned his image of Raze to his aid, he did so with his heart, not his body. Because in his heart, he knew none of this was right. It wasn't right for the cyborgs he couldn't reach or for the believers who regularly came to see him. One day, with Raze's help, he would fix everything he hated about this world. He just had to.

Chapter Four

Four days later

URIEL SMILED seductively, flipping his hair as he made his way toward Raze. *"Come on, lover,"* he whispered against Raze's lips as he rubbed his naked body against Raze's. *"Fuck me."*

Raze groaned as he allowed his hands to roam all over Uriel's nude form. Uriel's skin felt like silk under his fingertips, and his flowing blond hair fell over his shoulders in a perfect curtain of gold. His slender pink dick nudged Raze's own, triggering a maddening response in Raze, Jr.

Raze pushed Uriel down on the massive four-poster bed. In the blink of an eye, he got naked too and crawled on top of the beautiful young man. Uriel wrapped his arms around his neck and bit down on his ear, making Raze's dick throb. *"Raze,"* Uriel purred, *"please... I need you to—"*

Uriel didn't get to finish the phrase, because Raze cut him off with a kiss. Uriel moaned and parted his lips, eagerly granting Raze entrance. Raze thrust his tongue into Uriel's mouth, devouring the younger man, unable to sate his thirst for Uriel. He ground his cock against Uriel's, already aching to be buried inside Uriel's tight, welcoming body.

It wasn't enough, not nearly enough. Uriel must have thought the same, because he broke the kiss and shot Raze an inviting smile. "Come on, Raze. Feed me your cock. I know you want to."

Wordlessly, Raze straddled Uriel's chest and rubbed his cock over Uriel's lips, painting his lover's mouth with his precum. Uriel's pink tongue flicked out over the head of Raze's prick. Raze couldn't help but groan as Uriel's slick muscle teased him, stabbing into Raze's slit and making him ache for more. "Fuck," he grunted. "Yeah. Don't tease."

Burying his fingers in Uriel's hair, he thrust his dick into the other man's mouth. If Uriel was surprised, he didn't show it. He closed his eyes and released a muffled moan, like Raze's prick was a decadent treat, with Uriel being the rabid connoisseur devouring it. His throat worked convulsively around the glans, and he seemed to have foregone even the need to breathe, just so that he could suck Raze's dick.

More aroused than he ever remembered being, Raze started to fuck Uriel's mouth. The vibrations caused by Uriel's cries massaged his aching member, pooling into his balls, fueling the fire of Raze's lust. Just like Uriel had urged him to, Raze fed Uriel his dick, going faster and faster, heedless of the fact that he could be hurting Uriel, completely wild with desire.

He was so close now, already so close. He could feel his climax approaching, sizzling at the back of his spine, threatening to shut down his circuits. Hot, wet, raw, and carnal—it was a pursuit of pleasure at its most visceral.

And yet Raze couldn't reach satisfaction. His body was wired to crave Uriel in every way. His cock demanded to be sunk in Uriel's ass—and nothing else would do.

With great difficulty, Raze pulled his cock out of Uriel's mouth. Uriel pouted at being denied his prize, licking his puffy lips. "I hope you're going to find another place to put that magnificent prick."

Unable to look away from Uriel's beautiful face, Raze blindly reached for the lube dispenser. He procured some of the slick liquid and warmed it between his fingers. Meeting Uriel's lust-filled eyes, he reached between Uriel's asscheeks and slid a finger inside.

Uriel's body opened up to grant him entrance. The tight heat of Uriel's channel made Raze hiss. Already he could imagine how it would feel around his cock. Raze added another finger, scissoring them inside Uriel and finding his prostate. Uriel threw his head back and moaned, clinging to his shoulders and already impaling himself on Raze's digits. "Raze," he gasped out. "Now. I'm ready."

Raze couldn't take it anymore. Deeming Uriel as ready as he was going to get, Raze used a generous amount of the lubricant on his cock and lifted Uriel's legs onto his shoulders.

As he positioned his prick at Uriel's entrance, Uriel smiled at him again, his green eyes glittering with mischief. "Raze, I want to feel your cock inside me," he murmured seductively.

Just like that, Raze couldn't pretend anymore. Even with the mind-numbing need he experienced—or perhaps because of it—he pulled away from the Uriel look-alike and said, "Module shutdown. Computer, end VR session."

Immediately, Uriel's figure dissipated, as did the big bed. The dimly lit room vanished, melting into his quarters in the resistance hideout. Raze took off the VR goggles and threw them against the wall with a disgusted huff. Damn it. What had he been thinking, trying to use Logan's invention? He would never be satisfied with a copy of Uriel after he'd held the real thing in his arms.

"Well, hell." A familiar voice interrupted his self-deprecating musings. "It's not the fault of the machine you didn't enjoy yourself. Careful now."

Raze glowered at Logan, pissed off at himself that he hadn't noticed Logan's presence until he had spoken. "Can't I have some privacy here? In case you didn't notice, I was in the middle of something." He waved a hand in the general direction of his throbbing, unfortunate dick.

Logan ignored him. "Sorry," he replied blankly, crossing his arms over his chest as he leaned against the wall, not sounding very apologetic at all. "I was too curious to see what you thought about the VR."

Raze shook his head and left his bed, busying himself with getting dressed. Technically speaking, he hadn't needed to disrobe, but climaxing in the VR would have obviously caused a mess in real life too. Besides, the simple task gave Raze something to do. He took a couple of deep breaths and forced his prick into compliance, which was more difficult than it should have been. Finally, he pulled his clothes on, and when he was decent, he turned toward his friend. "What were you thinking when you programmed the damn thing? 'I want to feel your cock inside me,'" he parroted mockingly. "Seriously? Do you actually believe U— the Guiding Light would say something like that?"

"It doesn't matter if he would or not," Logan replied. "People like hearing the Guiding Light's voice talking dirty to them. We sell dreams, remember?"

Yes, Raze did remember, and he felt disgusted with himself for falling into it too. Since he'd returned to the ghettoes, though, he'd been haunted by Uriel's image, so much so that he hadn't been able to keep himself from entering Logan's VR. Right now he wanted nothing more than to destroy it. He'd never thought he'd feel guilty over something like this, but he could too easily lump himself with everyone else who exploited Uriel's beauty—who exploited him, period.

Oblivious to Raze's thoughts, Logan continued to speak. "I want to add some extra settings. That way, the customer can choose what attitude the Guiding Light should have. Seductive, coy, virginal—that sort of thing. I'll have you test it when it's ready."

Raze couldn't bear hearing any more. "I want to turn it off," he told his friend.

For a few moments, Logan stared at him and then exploded into bright peals of laughter. "Good one, Raze. Nice straight face. I almost believed you there."

"Believe it," Raze replied calmly. Fixing his friend with a steady look, he reiterated his words. "I want it off, as soon as possible. It's disrespectful."

Anger replaced the amusement on Logan's face. "Disrespectful?" he repeated, clenching and unclenching his fists. "How were the purists ever respectful of us? Jules told me you've been acting strange since you came back, but I didn't think…. Fuck. I didn't think he got to you so much."

"Yes, he did get to me," Raze admitted, "because I realized we were wrong about him."

"So you say." Logan snorted. "I'm increasingly skeptical about this expedition of yours. We're talking about the leader of the purists here. He can't be trusted. How do you know he's not just setting a trap for us? How can you be sure they didn't let you go so they can get to all of us?"

It was not the first time Logan had voiced his doubts over Raze's plan. He had originally intended to share the fact that Uriel was willing to help them with the rest of the resistance, but after testing the waters a bit, it had become obvious that they wouldn't be as open to Uriel's presence as Raze would have liked. That put Raze in the distinctly complicated position of not having informed other cyborgs—except Logan—of his idea. He wondered if it was even fair of him to expect Logan's support.

"You don't have to come with me," he told his friend. "It should be easy enough with the information I have."

Logan snorted. "Uh-huh. Like I'd let you go on a suicidal mission without me. Don't even think you can get rid of me."

Raze released a heavy sigh. He wished he could explain to Logan how he felt about Uriel, but he wasn't too sure himself. After a few days of being away from the man, a part of him had started to ask the same questions Logan had uttered.

Looking back at his one meeting with Uriel, he couldn't believe his own actions—how he'd trusted Uriel so blindly. It was so unlike him that he couldn't help but wonder whether Uriel had done something to influence his thought processes and emotions. He had told Uriel upfront that he belonged to the resistance, and Uriel hadn't even blinked. He'd let Uriel enter his mind and had lusted after him ever since the moment they'd first touched. And he'd asked Logan to shut down the VR club that practically funded the entire resistance.

It was probably unwise to pursue this, unwise to even go through with the plan. However, a part of him—the same one that had been dissatisfied with the Uriel look-alike in the module—screamed at him that what he'd felt with Uriel couldn't be a lie. Raze needed to know—because if he didn't pursue it, he would regret it for the rest of his life.

"I have to go, Logan," Raze told him. "He's the only chance my father has and... he's more than that. I can't explain it. I wish I could, but I'm not very sure I understand myself."

Logan clapped him on the shoulder. "Fair enough, my friend. You know I have your back, even when you want to do something terminally stupid. Just remember that if we do bring him to see your father, we have to be very careful."

Raze nodded. He did realize that—although he didn't look forward to explaining it to Uriel. "I'm aware of the risks, Logan. I wouldn't endanger the resistance. You have to know that."

"I do know. You've never led us astray so far, Raze. I'll follow your lead on this one too. But be ready, because not everyone will agree."

Raze rubbed his eyes tiredly. While as a leader he could reserve the right to make risky decisions and had done so in the past, he couldn't act of his own accord now. He couldn't just spring a visit from the Guiding Light on them, not only for the benefit of the members of the resistance—but for Uriel's as well.

"I suppose it's time to test that," he told his friend. "Gather the men, Logan. They should know what I have in mind."

Logan smiled grimly and left the room without another word. Raze was thankful for it, because he needed some time alone. He didn't remember ever feeling so shaken—not since the virus had first struck, destroying the very foundations of their society. He needed to get a grip, because otherwise, no matter what he'd told Logan, he would harm the resistance.

The thought did wonders to deflate his still-interested cock. They'd lost so much to the purists already. This expedition could change that—if Uriel was being honest—but it could also fuck things up even more.

He'd already scouted the location of Uriel's compound. He'd noted the rotation of the guards, which confirmed what he'd seen in Uriel's memories. Everything was in motion for tonight—and maybe, after seeing Uriel one more time, Raze would get the answers to his questions.

Raze ignored the way his still-human heart started to race at the thought and focused on the task ahead. He slid his fingers over a niche in the wall, and as the metal parted, it revealed a waiting suit of armor.

The armor was built from a special, nigh indestructible alloy that had been very popular before the virus had struck. It served as a replacement for the skin grafts some hard-core soldiers had chosen, which allowed them to be practically bulletproof. Since replacing his skin hadn't seemed like a good idea, Raze had chosen the armor. Unfortunately, after he'd lost the use of most of his implants, the thing had become too heavy to actually use in combat.

Raze stared at the armor for the longest time, wondering what message it would send should he decide to put it on. In the end, he mentally said a "fuck it." Whatever happened, whatever the rest of the resistance said, he would go after Uriel and he would bring him here. Of that he had no doubt. And all messages aside, the armor would serve as a useful tool should a confrontation happen between Raze's forces and the purist guards.

With no further hesitation, Raze quickly put the armor on, finding comfort in its solidity, in its weight over his shoulders and the knowledge that Uriel had made this possible. His doubts settled into a sense of clarity, and he straightened his shoulders as he finally left his quarters. His strange feelings for Uriel notwithstanding, this was the right thing to do.

Raze found most if not all of the members of the resistance gathered in the large corridor that formed the unofficial center of their base. Their murmurs reached his ears even as he descended the staircase that led to the right side of their living quarters. It was a little disconcerting at first, because he hadn't actually participated in a massive meeting like this since he'd gotten back the use of his implants. Their voices seemed louder, louder even than his improved senses should have made them.

"I wonder what this is all about," someone said.

"I have no idea," an older cyborg named Hugh replied. "Raze has been so mysterious since he went to that idiotic ceremony."

"I think he has a new plan to defeat the Guiding Light," a third one piped up.

Raze cleared his throat, and all eyes turned toward him. Several of those present gasped when they saw what Raze was wearing. Taking advantage of the silence, Raze began to speak.

"Some of you might be aware that, a few days ago, I attempted an incursion into purist territories. I know you've been wondering about the results of that incursion and about what I'm planning. Well, I have entered negotiations with the Guiding Light. I have reason to believe that he does, indeed, have genuine abilities, and he is willing to use them for our benefit."

The murmurs started anew.

"He's kidding, right?"

"He can't be serious."

"This is a joke."

"The Guiding Light is our enemy."

Raze met his brother's concerned eyes and smiled comfortingly at Julian—just a small twist of lips that only those who knew him well would see. Sobering, he proceeded to explain. "No, this is not a joke. I am perfectly serious. As you can see, I have regained the use of my implants, courtesy of the Guiding Light.

Tonight I will be meeting up with him and bringing him here, in the hope that he can help my father and all those suffering from CC-related afflictions."

Instantly, the area exploded into chaos. "I never thought I would say this, Raze," a woman named Odette called out to him, "but have you completely lost your mind?"

"Perhaps it's not irrationality," Hugh piped up. "Maybe it's far more comfortable to sell us out to the purists in exchange for so-called assistance."

Raze glowered at the older cyborg. Hugh had been a good friend of his father's before the virus had struck. At one point, Raze had come to consider the man his uncle. But when Raze had taken up the reins of the resistance, Hugh had slowly become resentful of having to defer to a man half his age, who had once played with drones and toy robots in front of him. It certainly didn't help that Hugh had once been one of the most sought-after doctors in the country but had become unable to perform even the most basic of medical tasks after the virus had struck. In a way, it stood to reason that Hugh would use this chance to undermine his authority, but Raze refused to accept it.

"You're awfully quick to brand me as a traitor," Raze pointed out. "Listen here, Hugh, and listen closely. This goes for everyone else here. I've led the resistance for years. I've never taken unjustifiable chances. This time around, I'm going to ask you to trust me. I realize this is a lot to take in, but I am not jumping into this rashly. Preparations have already been made for the expedition, and I assure you, we will not risk the safety of the resistance."

Logan chose this moment to intervene. "I stand behind Raze 100 percent. We all took chances simply by being here, by standing against the purists when they'd have us be their servants. We can't win without another leap of faith."

"Faith and risk are very different from stupidity and treason," Hugh pointed out bitingly.

"Hugh is right," Odette said, "but I've never known Raze to be either stupid or treasonous."

There were nods all around. "I don't trust the Guiding Light," someone else said, "but I trust Raze."

"If this works, it could provide us with a huge advantage over the purists."

Raze had expected doubt from his soldiers, and the overwhelming vote of confidence shocked him beyond belief. There were a few men and women who seemed less enthusiastic about it, but most of them cheered and immediately offered to come with him on the expedition.

Raze handpicked a few men and women whom he trusted to have his back and pulled them aside. "I've already done the preliminary scouting," he explained. "When night falls, we will be attacking the compound where the Guiding Light is held."

He didn't let his uncertainty show, but even as he spoke, he prayed the night would go well. He'd forgotten the last time he'd addressed a deity, but now seemed like a pretty good moment to go back to the habit. They certainly needed a bit of divine help. This wasn't just about Raze's father anymore, not really. Tonight the fate of the entire resistance lay in the balance. Success could win them leverage over the purist regime, the power to force them to adopt better policies for cyborgs. Failure could easily mean death.

But beyond that, tonight Raze would at last be reunited with Uriel. *Wait for me, Uriel. I'm coming.*

URIEL LAY curled on the bed, staring at the timepiece on the wall and watching the minutes drag by. The dim light emanating from the candles offered just enough visibility to register the excruciatingly slow progress.

The two ceremonial days had passed in a painful, humiliating blur. Consuming more libido suppressor had struck him hard, as had the violence in the agora. The only good thing that had come of it was that his mother hadn't badgered him too much upon his return to the compound. She'd allowed him to rest and recover from the effects of the fragrant oils, and this evening, she'd even left for a meeting with the rest of the Council.

All the pieces were in place. Uriel couldn't have asked for better circumstances for his escape. And yet now he was afraid.

It had seemed like a good idea at the time. Leaving the compound presented him with the opportunity of freedom and that of helping others who needed him. Raze had held him with such confidence and honesty. He'd opened his heart and mind to Uriel, and in turn, Uriel had rewarded him with the same trust.

However, as the days had passed, it occurred to Uriel that his powers weren't exactly reliable. Yes, he'd managed to grant relief to the people who'd come to see him, but what did that truly mean? He'd been unable to interpret any of the brief glimpses of memory he'd caught in Raze's mind. Truly, he did not know Raze at all— and yet he'd given the man open access to his life and destiny.

He felt so stupid and pathetic for clinging to the one person who had spoken his name in a promise, who saw past his identity as the Guiding Light. Much to his shame, he had to admit to himself that a part of his willingness to comply with Raze's terms was connected to his physical attraction to the man and the way it had felt to brush his fingers over Raze's stubbled cheek. Even now the memory made him tremble in arousal. His dick hardened, and he reached beneath his robes, gripping it in a tight fist.

In spite of knowing how wrong this was, Uriel rubbed his thumb over the leaking tip of his cock, biting his lower lip to muffle the cries he couldn't help. He used the precum already gathering over the glans to improve the glide, all the while imagining it was Raze's hand on him, Raze touching him and holding him.

Pleasure rushed over him as the memory of Raze's voice combined with his own frantic masturbation. He increased the speed of his strokes, all the while using his free hand to rub his oversensitive nipples. It felt so good it practically hurt, and Uriel kept going because he couldn't stop. His impending climax already burned in his testes, so close Uriel could practically taste it. And yet his body craved more. His anus clenched, aching for something Uriel barely dared to think about.

He'd never touched himself there, but courtesy of the informative imagery in the book he hadn't been able to finish, he knew how men coupled and what exactly it involved. When he'd read about it, he'd thought it sounded pretty painful, but after meeting Raze, he could easily imagine surrendering his body to him. Imagination let him indulge safely in what he couldn't have.

Continuing to jack himself off, he abandoned his nipples and trailed his fingers over his abdomen. In a last bid for modesty, he covered himself with a quilt, in case someone decided to burst in on him. When he was fairly certain of being safe from intrusive eyes, he settled on his back and spread his legs. Fully pushing his robes aside, he at last reached down and rubbed his finger over his nether opening.

He didn't know what he'd expected. According to the book, this was supposed to feel good. However, when Uriel tried to push his finger in, it seemed odd, awkward, and uncomfortable.

Uriel tried to remember what he'd done wrong, but his brain had become fuzzy with accumulated pleasure and piled-up uncertainties. Maybe he had it all wrong. Maybe it wasn't about a particular technique—but about who was doing the touching.

Instead of summoning the memory of the fictional love story between Scott and Eric, Uriel remembered that beautiful moment when he'd entered Raze's mind. Thrusting all doubts aside, he simply lost himself in the fantasy.

No longer hesitant, the hand on his dick—Raze's hand—found Uriel's most sensitive spots. Raze rubbed his fingers over Uriel's sac, then went back to the head of Uriel's dick. A thick, blunt finger pressed into Uriel's channel, and Raze's voice sounded in his ear. "Uriel…. Uriel."

When his orgasm came, it flowed over him unexpectedly, stemming from Raze's call and his own need to be one with the other man. Uriel's pleasure peaked, and with a cry he couldn't smother, he fell over the edge. His cock throbbed and pulsed, shooting streaks of hot cum all over his chest and the blanket.

For a few moments it felt completely right, and Uriel had no doubt that he was supposed to be with Raze in every single way possible. And then, as the high of the pleasure began to fade, it settled into a cold realization and a loneliness that couldn't be denied. Raze wasn't here, and even if he had been, Uriel shouldn't be considering intercourse with a virtual stranger.

Uriel stumbled out of the bed and into the adjoining bath chamber. He quickly wiped the traces of his orgasm from his skin, embarrassed and ashamed at his behavior. A few minutes earlier, he'd berated himself for being so trusting, and now he'd masturbated over the consequences of that naiveté. Would his foolishness never cease?

When he returned to his quarters, Uriel pulled on new, fresh robes and accepted the truth. He couldn't truly berate himself for trusting Raze, because his heart—and okay, maybe his libido too—told him he'd made a good decision. But this wasn't only about him. Things simply couldn't continue this way, and Raze would help Uriel to start the change. He just hoped that, when Raze finally arrived, he'd know that for sure.

Uriel double-checked the lock on his door, knowing that if things went wrong he might need it. As a rule, he wasn't allowed to use it, but this time around he might have to.

Once he made sure everything was in order, Uriel lay back on the bed and settled himself in for a long wait. *Come for me, Raze*, he thought. *Come for me.*

Chapter Five

THE COMPOUND where the Guiding Light lived—or was imprisoned, depending on who you asked—reminded Raze of one of those fortresses in the documentaries his father had once forced him to watch. An underground bunker, it had a limited number of entries and exits, all of which were permanently watched by guards. The natural green beauty of the compound outskirts hid hundreds of sensors that could detect any approaching intruder if they even breathed nearby.

However, Uriel knew more than the compound builders realized—maybe even than he himself thought. With Uriel's memories put together, Raze had found the weak spot of the stronghold.

A few miles from the actual compound, a hidden passage opened to the supply route used to transport everything from food and clothing for the Guiding Light to weaponry for the purists stationed there.

It was to this passageway that Raze had led his men. They sneaked into the area, carefully settling blocking cages between a handful of sensors. The devices engulfed the sensors in miniature plasma shields that cut off the feed without triggering any automated alarms. They would keep Raze and his men safe for a few minutes, before the security of the main compound realized the problem.

Thankfully, Raze knew when the transport would arrive—shortly after the Guiding Light retreated to his quarters.

Ten o'clock. Two hours to midnight. That was the precise time when the doors would slide open, allowing Raze and his small group inside. At least that was what needed to happen for everything to go without a hitch.

At five minutes to ten, no vehicle had arrived. Logan shot him a telling look but said nothing. Raze nodded in turn, acknowledging his friend's unspoken words. Yes, he knew it was dangerous, but he wouldn't back out of this, not yet. Now that he was there, he felt even more compelled to burst into the damn compound, to touch Uriel and finally free the man.

At two minutes to the established hour, a large hovercraft approached. In front of them, a huge hatch opened to allow the entrance of the aircraft. Raze lifted his hand and counted to five, using his fingers. When he reached the final digit, he leaped onto the roof of the vehicle. Logan and their four companions followed, landing on the smooth surface with barely a sound.

Raze held his breath, waiting for any reaction or a sign that they'd been detected. For infiltration operations, they used special boots that kept them from making noise, but if anyone inside the hovercraft was paying attention, they might have heard the sound of them hitting the roof—which couldn't be helped.

Thankfully, this didn't seem to be the case, and Raze guessed the hum of the engine must have blocked the noise he and his team had made. The hovercraft entered the hatch with no incident while Raze dropped on his belly and waited. They might be inside, but the hard part was only starting.

The transport corridor was protected by several doors that could only be accessed through certain codes. Thankfully, Uriel had been through here once, the first day he'd come to live at the compound. He'd been asked to bless the premises, and in the process had noted the codes with that distant, absentminded type of observation most people registered random faces and things they ran into throughout the course of their day-to-day lives. If asked, he'd have probably sworn he had no idea what the codes could be, but Raze's mental computer had managed to retrieve the information regardless.

The problem was that Raze didn't know if the codes would work. They could have been changed since then—in fact, chances of the same codes remaining active were slim at best. If Plan A didn't work, he'd have to force the real codes out of the staff, and for Uriel's benefit, he would prefer not to resort to deadly force.

As it turned out, the personnel here seemed almost oddly lax. The pilot descended from the hovercraft, bobbing his head in the rhythm of a tune he was listening to on his headset. He met up with some bored-looking guards, who proceeded to unload the cargo without much interest.

Raze shared a look with Logan, who grimaced, obviously feeling odd about the entire thing as well. "Trap," he mouthed at Raze.

As much as Raze hated to admit it, the attitude of the purist guards was suspicious at best. But Raze didn't want to think Uriel would stab him in the back like this. Remembering Uriel's innocent green eyes, he refused to consider it. As foolish as it might have seemed, he would follow through with the promise he'd made to Uriel. But he couldn't expect Logan and the others to follow him into danger. This was his fight in the end, and Uriel had trusted him—not anyone else.

"Wait here," he told his friend. "I won't be long."

Logan's eyes widened. "Raze, no," he started to say, "you can't...."

"If anything happens, you'll know."

Raze caught a moment during which the guards were turned away and leaped off the hovercraft. Against all odds, he slipped past them, which perpetuated his belief that something was awfully wrong.

As the group busied themselves with transporting the goods, Raze snuck into the passageway. He reached the first door without running into additional guards. Presumably, they were participating in unloading the supplies. Raze found the control pad and quickly punched in the code. He didn't know if he was relieved or disheartened when it worked like a charm.

His body tensing in preparation for combat, Raze advanced through the corridor. A few hundred feet in, a group of guards blocked his path. The passageway was too cramped, keeping him from using stealth to fool them. He'd have to bypass them the old-fashioned way.

Just like the men before, the guards seemed completely relaxed, as if they didn't think anything could possibly go wrong. Two of them were sharing a drink, while others were bent over a traditional game of cards. Raze almost wanted to snort. He'd never been able to understand the purists. Except for security measures, they shunned the latest in technology. Purist medical care and entertainment had returned to the state of centuries ago. Ironically, it gave Raze and the resistance the upper hand in terms of tech.

Not that Raze minded. As suspicious as he might be of the guards' motives and behavior, he took his chance. Moving faster than the human eye could see, Raze attacked. He delivered certain well-placed blows, knocking the men out without hurting them unnecessarily. One of the guards released a startled cry and tried to reach for an alarm button. He never got the chance to hit it. Raze pinned him to the wall and head butted him. The purist's eyes rolled in his head, and he slumped against Raze.

Even seeing the man's slight resistance, Raze didn't feel particularly impressed by purist security, and neither was he surprised when the code for the second door worked as well.

Raze repeated the process a few more times, advancing deeper, closer to his destination. Finally, he reached the last door, the one that led into the main compound. The moment he bypassed it, he found himself facing about twenty phaser pistols, armed and pointed his way.

"Stop right there, cyborg," one of the older guards shouted. "Did you really think you could infiltrate the Guiding Light's home so easily?"

Raze craned his neck and threw the man a grin. "This is hardly a home. It's more like a prison."

The man—whom Raze assumed must be some sort of leader there—glowered at Raze, his face going as red as the circuits of a cyborg whore. "What would you know of it, machine-man? We protect the Guiding Light's purity from degenerates and freaks like you."

Raze didn't bother listening to any more of the self-righteous babble. He'd heard it countless times in the propaganda of the purists and had witnessed it through Uriel's memories. Maybe the man truly believed what he was saying, but Raze couldn't care less.

He brought up his armor's menu within his mind. "Computer, activate battle mode."

"Battle mode activated," the disembodied voice reported. "All systems operational."

Instantly, his armor spread all over his body, encasing every part of him in the alloy. The older guards stared at him, frozen as they realized what had happened. The younger ones began shooting, the bolts of energy hitting Raze without even making a dent in the armor. They were probably just a little older than Uriel, and they didn't remember what kind of equipment professional cyborg soldiers could use. The metal itself might not have withstood the full extent of the blast without Raze feeling the pain, but the armor had additional plasma shields similar to the ones used by spaceships— although of course not quite of that magnitude.

If the young purists didn't know about it, Raze would gladly teach them this lesson and refresh the memory of the older men in the process. Unwilling to stand around to chat, he shot into action. Going on the age-old but still valid principle of "you show me yours, I'll show you mine," he activated his own phaser. The weapon emerged from the actual armor, bound to Raze's wrist and easily controllable through Raze's mental computer. He shot several energy blasts at the group but not before he set the intensity of it on "stun," since again, he had no intention of killing the purists.

By now the alarms were blaring, and Raze knew he didn't have much time left. The computer chose this exact moment to notify him, "Plasma shields down to 80 percent capacity."

Raze stopped playing around and took everyone out in a few quick moves. He couldn't afford to linger for much longer—his men might be skilled, but they didn't have the professional equipment Raze did. Not to mention that the purists could try to move Uriel from this location, and Raze simply couldn't allow that.

He started running in the direction of Uriel's quarters, going up several flights of stairs—elevators were a no-no here—running into other guards and taking them out as well. All the while, his mental computer guided his steps, providing him with a 3-D map of the facility.

At last he reached his destination and, predictably, ran into a disheartening number of guards. Well, they didn't actually see him, at least not at first, since he stopped right before he entered the corridor. That didn't change the fact that there were more than thirty men blocking the path to Uriel's quarters. Meanwhile, a middle-aged purist dressed in a butler's outfit insistently knocked at Uriel's door. "I understand that you're afraid, Your Holiness," the man said, "but you mustn't be concerned. We're here for your protection. We won't allow the attackers to lay a finger on you."

No reply came from inside. A guard lingering next to the butler nudged him with his elbow. "Can we move this along, Phelps? If we don't leave now, I can't guarantee his safety."

"What would you have me do?" Phelps snapped at him. "His Holiness barricaded himself inside. You should have never allowed things to reach this point in the first place."

"We didn't expect cyborgs with CCs over the regularly functional limit. Never mind. Just break down the door. We have to retrieve the Guiding Light."

"If only it were that easy," Phelps answered. "You know as well as I do that it's solid, reinforced tungsten alloy."

"Well, then we'd better start," the chief guard replied.

Tungsten, huh? Well, this was an interesting development. Taking into account the pale faces of everyone he could see, they all knew—like Raze did—they would need a plasma cannon to bring down that door. Coincidentally, the solid metal resembled Raze's armor. The guards couldn't possibly enter Uriel's quarters if Uriel refused to allow them inside.

Of course, this also meant Raze couldn't get in either. He officially branded the purists as idiots. Uriel was safer behind that door than anywhere else, and if he'd truly been a cyborg assassin, he'd have been stuck and unable to touch his target. Not to mention that they seemed to think he'd brought his men along—which wasn't the case. The gist of it was that they should have kept Uriel in his quarters, not tried to get him out.

Unlike the purist guards, Raze had hope that Uriel would open the door for him. And so he proceeded to remove the last barrier between him and Uriel: the men themselves.

Taking a deep breath, Raze launched himself into battle. Their idiocy aside, these particular guards seemed better trained than the others, and once they saw him, they instantly turned toward him. They didn't bother with hand-to-hand combat like previous soldiers had and instead went straight for their phasers—shooting to kill.

Raze dodged several blasts, but some of them did hit true and would have likely incapacitated if not killed him had he not worn his armor. As it was, his mental computer began to beep alarmingly as his plasma shields dropped below 50 percent.

Cursing, Raze swept through his opponents, crushing their weapons in his fist. At last the only ones remaining were Phelps the butler and the guard leader.

"You won't get past me, you monster," the purist soldier snarled.

Raze didn't bother to address that. He dodged the plasma blast from the other man with ease and punched him in the face, sending him flying against the wall. Remarkably, even when the last soldier lost consciousness, Phelps didn't flee. He straightened his back and physically positioned himself in front of the door.

"If you want the Guiding Light, you're going to have to go through me."

Raze released a mental sigh. Why was it that these brave fools thought their courage would make a difference? It never did, not really. That was one lesson Raze had learned both before and after the virus had struck. Courage didn't mean squat if one didn't have the strength to back it up. Some would have argued that courage itself was a victory, but that sort of thing only counted for dreamers, not for people like Raze, who fought every single day and still had to watch his father slowly withering away.

The butler's efforts might have been laudable, and Raze appreciated the purists' loyalty to their Guiding Light. Unfortunately, like everyone here, it wasn't Uriel he protected but the putrid system that had enslaved their own so-called leader.

"And what makes you think I wouldn't kill you to get to him?" he asked.

"I don't matter," the man insisted, completely missing the point. "Only the Guiding Light does."

Raze peered a little closer at the man's face. He featured in quite a lot of Uriel's memories, although Raze couldn't be sure if his obsessive behavior could be considered worrisome or not. Interestingly, Raze remembered him from a time when he'd been far more than a butler. At one point, Raze's father had actually worked for the man. How ironic.

Well, in any case, that life was gone for Phelps, because he'd become completely resolute in the belief that the Guiding Light mattered more than anything else. Much to his own dismay, Raze understood him a little. Although his image of Uriel was quite different, he could almost empathize with Phelps.

But Raze had a job to do, and he'd do it no matter what Phelps tried. "Maybe you're right," he said, "but sadly, you can't change what happens to him from now on."

He was just about to forcibly push the man aside, when the metallic sound of a mechanism being triggered interrupted the conversation. The massive door opened, revealing Uriel standing beyond it.

Unshed tears filled his eyes, and he whispered, "Stop this. Please."

Phelps gasped. "No, Your Holiness. You mustn't sacrifice yourself for me. You're too important."

In Uriel's tight smile, Raze saw a guilt that, shockingly, echoed the one inside him. When Raze reached for him, Uriel shied away. He gasped at the sight of the fallen bodies of his men. "Oh, no. What have I done?"

Raze couldn't let Uriel think the purist guards were dead, but now was not the time or the place to clarify the situation. Pushing past Phelps, Raze took Uriel in his arms and draped him over his shoulder.

Phelps tried to protest, but Raze was already running, heading toward the corridors once again. Uriel said nothing, but his body went rigid as they advanced and he took in the apparent devastation Raze had left behind.

Raze had every intention of explaining, once they were safe and preferably a good distance away from the compound. He guessed being encased in the armor didn't help matters, but he couldn't take it off yet.

As it turned out, he should have reorganized his priorities differently. Raze's hearing registered an alarming increase in Uriel's breathing and heart rate. Raze immediately put him down, realizing that Uriel was having a panic attack.

"Hush now, baby," Raze started to say, reaching for Uriel's smooth cheek. "I promise you, I—"

The moment his fingers came into contact with Uriel's flesh, a jolt of energy exploded through Raze. Raze's nerve endings didn't get the chance to register any pain. In fact, he didn't even realize what had happened until his mental computer rebooted.

"System initiation," it said. "Recovery from critical error complete."

Sometimes Raze really hated that blasted voice. He didn't know who'd thought it amusing to give mental computers a separate vocal identity, but he didn't agree with their assessment at all. For crying out loud, Raze could tell that the system was initiating on his own, without being told so.

Raze shook himself and focused on finding Uriel. He didn't have to look very hard. His Guiding Light—and when had he started thinking of Uriel as his, anyway?—knelt next to him, his blond hair in disarray, his eyes still swollen and filled with too much sadness. "I'm so sorry, Raze," Uriel said. "I didn't mean to hurt you."

"It's okay, baby." Raze rubbed his eyes to clear away the dizziness and realized his helmet had retracted. That was a good thing, because now he got an unhindered look at Uriel's beautiful face. "My fault. I should have realized you would be hurt if you thought I'd killed them. And no, they're not dead. I just knocked them out. I assure you they'll be perfectly fine."

Uriel lit up, and his bright smile left Raze dumbstruck and more than a little aroused. "And I should have known you would do that. I'm such an idiot."

Except he wasn't, not at all. Like Raze, Uriel had obviously been plagued by uncertainties, not knowing if he'd done the right thing to trust a virtual stranger. In some ways, the two of them were as alike as they were different.

Raze stared at Uriel, wanting nothing more than to kiss him, to hold him close and assure him he was safe. Sadly, practicality once more demanded his attention. "We should go, Uriel," Raze said as he got up. "I want us to be long gone by the time these guys wake up."

Uriel nodded, and although his eyes still held a touch of uncertainty, he came to Raze willingly. Raze picked Uriel up, this time carrying him in his arms like he would a lover. They encountered no obstacle of the human sort on their trip toward the exit, but that didn't mean it was easy. The compound security had finally gotten off their

73

asses. Security doors that hadn't been there were sliding shut behind them, like an angry, possessive beast snapping its jaws at them in an attempt to retrieve the prize it zealously guarded. Raze ran faster than he had in his entire life and managed to enter the supply corridor instants before a heavy tungsten door blocked the way in.

Distantly, Raze wondered why the purists hadn't done that before. There had been plenty of time during which they could have trapped Raze inside while he was engaged in combat. But if something suspicious was going on, Raze couldn't unearth it yet. First he had to unearth himself, Uriel, and his men out of this hellhole.

When he reached his point of entry—which, unfortunately, had to be his point of exit as well—he found Logan and the others waiting for him, having already taken command of the hovercraft. The guards were knocked out or tied up, since Raze had given his group specific instructions to avoid the use of deadly force.

Even if they'd followed Raze's orders to the letter, the other cyborgs still gaped in shock upon seeing him. Technically speaking, Uriel, not Raze, was one they were staring at. Hearing about Raze's plan to steal the Guiding Light hadn't prepared them for its actual consequences, for seeing Uriel firsthand.

Uriel tensed in Raze's arms but said nothing, suddenly finding Raze's chin a very interesting spot to study. Raze knew a different battle was ahead, one that involved doubts and prejudice instead of flying fists and phasers. He wished he could have spared Uriel the heartache, but it was out of his hands. He didn't have time to address the concerns of his soldiers either. "Board the hovercraft," he ordered. "Quickly. We have to get out of here, now."

No one asked any questions, instead complying with the command. Logan settled in the pilot seat, while the others took care of the remaining preparations for takeoff. Meanwhile, Raze secured Uriel in the most comfortable seat he could find. It wasn't easy—Uriel's hair got in the way, since Raze hadn't had the foresight to ask Uriel to bind it back. Uriel seemed experienced with handling it, because he settled it in his lap with little fuss. He hadn't looked at Raze since they'd boarded the ship, and that worried Raze.

At last the hovercraft obeyed Logan's commands and they took off. Raze took advantage of the brief respite to address his charge. "Hey. You all right?"

Uriel looked up. "Yes," he replied softly. "Just… nervous, I suppose."

Raze knelt in front of Uriel and, on impulse, reached for the younger man's hands. The moment they touched, that bolt of electricity shot through Raze again, but this time he didn't black out. Instead, his cock went rock hard again, straining uncomfortably against the material of his undergarments.

Gritting his teeth, he focused on offering Uriel a comforting smile. "I can understand that," he replied, choosing honesty as the one thing that could soothe Uriel. "It's been hard to trust that we're doing the right thing. I admit I've been fretting and musing over it too."

Uriel squeezed Raze's palm so tightly that Raze almost regretted having retracted his armored gloves—almost, but not quite. "I'm afraid," Uriel admitted, "afraid that I acted selfishly just so that I could be free. I was so scared that I'd convinced myself to trust you because I couldn't carry the burden of being the Guiding Light any longer."

Raze's heart clenched at the near desperation in Uriel's voice. Even knowing they were being watched, Raze couldn't help but embrace Uriel. They hardly knew each other, but they'd both thrown all caution to the wind when they'd met. That had to mean something, although Raze didn't dare guess what it could be.

"We're in this together, Uriel," he whispered. "You're not alone. You'll never be alone again."

Uriel's breath caught, and he buried his face in Raze's neck. It couldn't have been very comfortable, given that Raze still wore most of his armor. In fact, their skin didn't actually make contact. Dissatisfied, Raze sent a mental command to his computer, retracting the metal to its smallest form.

Uriel seemed to appreciate that a lot, because his hold on Raze tightened. He didn't quite touch Raze—that was far too intimate for this setting, and it probably would have made Uriel uncomfortable.

Nevertheless, his breath tickled Raze's neck, and Raze really shouldn't have liked that as much as he did.

Before he knew it, he found himself pulling Uriel even closer, wanting nothing more than to kiss him. He'd have probably done exactly that, but Logan chose that moment to intervene.

"I hate to interrupt this touching episode," Logan said, "but we're almost to our ship."

Uriel broke away from Raze, and the loss of his literally electrifying touch stirred something angry inside Raze. He took a deep breath and got up, facing his friend with what he hoped was a calm demeanor. "Thank you, Logan," he replied.

Logan arched a brow, which made Raze guess that his carefully cultivated mask wasn't that believable after all. He cleared his throat and looked from Raze to Uriel, then back to Raze. "We're going to have to search him," he said. "He could have tracking devices on him."

Uriel released a soft gasp, and on impulse, Raze shielded Uriel with his own body. Logan had a point, of course. Raze had promised to be careful with how they approached Uriel's presence in the headquarters of the resistance. He'd been so worried about assuring his people they didn't need to fear a thing that he'd forgotten or dismissed what it would entail for Uriel.

"I'll do it," he told Logan. "No one else touches him but me."

"Raze...." Logan started to protest. "No offense, but you seem emotionally involved with him. Maybe it would be best if I—"

Raze glowered at his friend and interrupted Logan before the other man could finish the phrase. "I said I'll do it. Don't start something with me, Logan. I don't want to fight you."

"Jesus, Raze, can you hear yourself?" Logan slowly backed away. "We've been friends for years. What in the world are you doing?"

If he were perfectly honest, Raze himself didn't know. He might have completely overreacted to Logan's words, but just the idea of someone touching Uriel had the circuits of his mental computer crackling ominously.

He took a deep breath, struggling for calm. He couldn't understand his own emotions anymore, and that didn't bode well for his ability to lead. "Uriel wouldn't jeopardize the resistance, and neither would I. Like I said, I will check."

Logan still didn't look convinced, and the situation might have escalated dangerously had Uriel not gotten in the way. "It's okay, Raze," Uriel said as he got up. "His distrust is understandable. What would you like me to do?"

"You'll have to disrobe," Logan explained. "We don't have the tech to perform a noninvasive scan here, so there'll be some discomfort on your part, but I'm afraid it can't be helped."

Uriel went ashen. Raze appreciated the effort, but he knew how difficult it had been for Uriel to accept his touch. There was no way he'd allow Logan to go through with a search that could be painful for Uriel.

"I have the use of my implants back," he said tightly, "and even if I didn't, I can scan him. There's no need for unpleasantness."

Logan said nothing else, but his jaw clenched as he glared at Uriel. It was obvious that, for all his words, he didn't trust Raze as much as he'd claimed. And okay, maybe Raze had messed up in displaying such affection toward a man whom most cyborgs considered their worst enemy, but he couldn't regret it, not really. Even if it had led Logan to doubt him, it felt right to comfort Uriel like this.

"Come on," Raze told Uriel. "Let me look you over. Do you think you have any tracking devices implanted?"

Uriel shook his head. "It is forbidden. I don't spend much time around modern technology at all. I don't even wear artificial clothing. I'm required to be pure."

"Right," Logan drawled. "And you wouldn't happen to know why security at your compound was so poor?"

Uriel frowned. "Was it? I... I couldn't really tell. I mean... it could be because my mother left for a meeting with the rest of the Council. Usually, postceremonial periods are slow for me, because I need some time to recover after the effort of the days spent in Genesis. So maybe none of them expected an attack. I can't imagine another reason."

Raze took in Uriel's explanation, all the while using his newly working implants to scan Uriel for any tracking devices. Uriel was right. The garments he wore seemed to be woven using ancient, traditional methods that Raze had considered extinct a long time ago. The material didn't hold any artificial compounds either, and very few foreign bodies. Raze had never seen cleaner clothes in his life.

"You're not carrying anything suspicious, but just to be safe, we'll leave your garments here. We brought you something of ours you can wear."

"What about internal implants?" Logan inquired.

"There's nothing," Raze told his friend. His mental computer would have picked up the signal or even the presence of a detection implant inside Uriel's body.

Unsurprisingly, Logan still eyed Uriel with distrust and apprehension. Uriel straightened his shoulders and stared back at him. "I understand that you don't like me. I can't do anything to change that. But while you're trying to find suspicious motivations in my every action, please consider who I am. I am the Guiding Light. I highly doubt the Council would just hand me over, even to capture the entire resistance. Also, before meeting Raze, the only other person I'd touched in my life was my mother. You will excuse me if I'm not too eager to allow an invasive cavity search."

Logan arched a brow, perhaps not expecting the so-far quiet Uriel to snap at him. "But we only have your word on that, now don't we?"

"If you don't believe me, you can always drop me nearby," Uriel pointed out. "I'm not forcing anyone to bring me anywhere. I only wanted to help, because I am told people are dying. If you hate me too much to deem my assistance adequate, feel free to refuse it."

"Spare me the self-righteousness," Logan spat back. "I don't know how you got Raze to believe your propaganda, but I won't fall into your little scheme. We do have scanning machines at HQ, and I'll be watching you."

"Fair enough," Uriel answered. "I don't blame you for that."

Logan opened his mouth like he wanted to say something else—perhaps just so that Uriel wouldn't have the last word. Raze scowled at his friend, and Logan huffed. He turned on his heel and angrily stalked back to the pilot seat, starting to make the maneuvers for their landing.

As soon as Logan was gone, Uriel's shoulders slumped and he offered Raze a tired, apologetic smile. "I'm sorry. I didn't mean to get you into a fight with your friend."

Raze shook his head. "I'm the one who should apologize. I didn't consider the implications of taking you to see my father, not until after we'd already come up with the plan. All of us in the resistance have suffered a great deal because of the purists, and their distrust will naturally fall onto you."

"And yet, here you are." Uriel eyed Raze with a speculative gleam in his beautiful green eyes. "I'm starting to wonder now, just what position you occupy in the resistance."

Raze sighed heavily. "I think you already know, don't you?"

Uriel nodded but didn't seem particularly worried. After a brief moment of hesitation, he reached for Raze's hand. "Leader or no, I think we're in this together now. And I'm not sorry I trusted you. Not anymore."

Raze ached to kiss those lovely full lips that only seemed to twist into a genuine smile for him. However, he became aware that they were close to the area where they'd stashed their vessel.

Sliding away some of the seats, he retrieved one of the few packs they'd brought along. "Go ahead and change," he said. "We don't have much time left."

Uriel nodded and started to undo his robes. Raze's mind almost shut down. For obvious reasons, Uriel wasn't particularly self-conscious about his nudity. That was going to be a problem for Raze's concentration, because Uriel's naked body starred in most—cancel that, in all—of Raze's recent sexual fantasies.

Raze turned around, blocking everyone else's sight of Uriel with his own body. His men threw a few gazes his way, obviously not knowing what to believe anymore. None of them argued with him, likely guessing that if Logan hadn't managed to get through to him, the rest of them would have even less success. They were probably lucky in that regard, since Raze's arousal didn't improve his mood. He twitched slightly when Uriel released a small, startled whimper. "Everything okay?" he asked.

"Yes," Uriel answered. "It's just... I'm not used to clothing like this."

A few moments later, Uriel's soft hand tapped Raze's shoulder. Raze turned and was greeted with the most beautiful sight in existence. Free of the robes that marked him as the Guiding Light, Uriel nevertheless reminded Raze of the angels mankind had once believed in and tried to emulate. Okay, so the thoughts Uriel conjured in Raze's mind weren't very angelic in nature, but who could blame him? With his long hair mussed and his face flushed from the slight exertion, Uriel looked more beautiful than ever and definitely more touchable—which was really the last thing Raze needed. The tight cut of the clothing also emphasized every line of Uriel's toned form, and Raze's hands itched to reach out to him.

"Well?" Uriel asked with one of those beautiful, heart-stopping smiles. "What do you think?"

URIEL WASN'T sure how to interpret Raze's reaction to his new garments. Even after he inquired into it, Raze didn't immediately answer. Uriel wondered if he looked so ridiculous that Raze didn't want to hurt his feelings. He certainly felt awkward. The tall boots he now wore bit his sensitive legs, and the breeches felt far more restraining than his robes ever had. Similarly, the upper garment hugged his chest like a second skin, making Uriel impossibly aware of his own body… and somewhat itchy. In fact, he had to bite the inside of his cheek to keep himself from scratching a particular spot on his lower back.

After what seemed like forever, Raze cleared his throat. "You look great. Leave your clothes there. We're abandoning the ship."

"I think a more adequate phrasing is crashing it," Raze's friend, Logan, piped up from behind Raze. "Now come on. I already set it on a collision course for the closest hill."

"Have you looked through the supplies in the cargo hold?" Raze inquired, suddenly all business.

Logan nodded. "There's some medicine and weaponry we could use, but they're all marked with the seal of the Council. It'd be easily detectable in a sweep."

"Leave it, then," Raze ordered. As alarms started to blare, everyone shot into action, equipping themselves for the crash.

Uriel stood there, not knowing what to do. His first experience with actual violence had been tonight, during Raze's attack on the compound. Now they were crashing the aircraft, and for the first time in his life, Uriel experienced a very real sense of fear.

He hadn't considered the full extent of how this would affect his life, and for all his bravado, he wasn't in the slightest bit ready to face the mistrust of the cyborgs—or their way of life.

Fortunately, Raze seemed to read his mind. "Just stick with me," he whispered. "Nothing bad is going to happen. I promise."

With the same ease Uriel would have in combing his hair—or maybe easier—Raze lifted him in his arms like he had in the compound. "Hold onto me," he told Uriel.

Uriel complied. He'd always hated feeling helpless and out of his depth, and he hated it now—but trying to prove himself to Raze at this particular moment would be just plain idiotic. And so he clung to Raze's neck, held his breath, and put his trust in the man he'd followed into the unknown.

Logan slid the door of the hovercraft open. Frigid air combined with exhaust fumes assaulted Uriel. He coughed, unused to the smell of the burned fuels. His family always came to pick him up through the traditional method of a horse and carriage—and Uriel could definitely see the advantage now.

Raze noted the thick fumes with a thoughtful hum. "You failed to mention that you'd wrecked the engine, Logan."

Logan grinned at them. "Yes, well, I figured you'd notice."

Without giving Raze a chance to reply, Logan jumped out of the aircraft. Raze followed, and Uriel smothered a yell as they started to fall. He would not scream. He refused to be cowardly. He'd go through with this to the end, no matter what happened.

"Close your eyes," Raze told him, "and listen to my voice."

As Uriel did, Raze continued to speak, "I want to promise you something, Uriel. I've told you before that I'm so grateful that you trusted me and you were willing to leave everything behind to help us. I told you I would take care of you, and nothing is going to harm you. I meant all that. But when this is all over, I want to tell you more, everything you mean to me and everything you've given me."

Raze set Uriel down, and Uriel opened his eyes, realizing he'd been so focused on Raze's words he hadn't registered they'd stopped falling. From the corner of his eye, he caught sight of the hovercraft crashing into the hill and exploding upon contact. Raze's companions landed next to Uriel, at which point Uriel realized they were all equipped with jetpacks. He felt like an idiot, because he should have known Raze had technology that would keep them from actually making unpleasant contact with the ground.

Logan was already unveiling another aircraft from a stealth shield of sorts. Everyone boarded, and Raze guided Uriel inside. In the distance, Uriel could already hear other vehicles approaching, likely people from the compound looking for them.

Somehow Uriel knew it was far too late for anyone to reach them, and his guess was confirmed moments later, when upon takeoff, Logan released a victorious whoop. "All right! We gave them the slip."

In his enthusiasm, he almost seemed to have forgotten about his anger with Uriel, but of course that was too much to ask for. Even from his pilot seat, Logan threw an ugly look Uriel's way. "Of course that might prove to be useless if a certain someone on the ship—"

"It won't be useless," Uriel interrupted the other man. "I wouldn't betray my promise to Raze."

"It's not your promise I'm relying on, Guiding Light. I know that in the end, if you do stab us in the back, my friend will do the right thing."

"I'm sure it won't be necessary," Raze replied. He squeezed Logan's shoulder and added, "Come on. Let's head out. Julian and my father are waiting."

Uriel settled down in a seat and buckled in, preparing himself for what would undoubtedly be an eventful ride. The ship was quite tiny—half the size of the hovercraft—and even with Logan's skillful guidance, it seemed to flip and screech as it flew through the air. Uriel's stomach roiled, but he found that place in his mind that helped him throughout the never-ending ceremonial days. Suddenly, withstanding the rocking of the ship wasn't so hard anymore. After two days of slow, humiliating torture, he could welcome a little excitement.

He remembered Raze's words, his promise of revealing what Uriel meant to him. His heart started to beat a little faster as he considered that Raze might feel the same thing Uriel did. Truly, Uriel himself wasn't sure how he felt. Still, whatever it was that made him warm inside when he thought of Raze gave him courage to face these new challenges.

It occurred to him then that he hadn't actually discussed with Raze what would happen after Uriel helped Raze's people. The Council wouldn't let this slide. They would track Uriel down to the ends of earth, and anyone who stood in their way would suffer the consequences.

A chill went down Uriel's spine, and he reached for Raze's arm. "I have to go back. After we do this, I need to return there.

They'll never believe that I'm dead, and even if they do, the retaliation will be horrible."

"They were already hunting us and have been for years," Raze replied matter-of-factly. "None of us in the resistance are afraid of the Council. However, we have prepared a message we will send to the purists, assuring your safety as long as they fulfill our demands. In a way, that's the whole point. We don't even want them to believe you're dead, but if they think we're keeping you prisoner, they might acquiesce to some of our requests."

For all his words, he didn't deny Uriel's statement of having to return to his previous life. He reached for Uriel's hand and squeezed it tightly, like he didn't want to let go ever again. Seeing the turmoil in the other man's deep black eyes, Uriel offered him a tiny, comforting smile. He wanted to tell Raze that he was sure they'd find a solution, but that would have been a lie. Instead, he said, "The Council will never risk any harm coming to me, so for now, you have the advantage. Let's take everything one step at a time. We'll help your father and then decide what to do."

No one else spoke, at least not through words. The heavy silence that fell over the aircraft told Uriel that all those present were aware of the implications of Uriel's visit. Yes, the resistance had made a huge step ahead by supposedly kidnapping Uriel, but that didn't mean things would become easier from now on. As for Uriel.... The most he could hope for was to be what Raze needed and save the man's father.

He pushed back all thoughts of finding possible happiness with Raze. What he needed to do now was to focus on helping the cyborgs, so that when he went back to the Council, he could approach them with a real proposition to change the way things worked. They were all people. Cyborgs or purists, they needed to work together for the benefit of mankind. And maybe Uriel had been a tool all his life, but that had changed when he met Raze. He wanted to make a difference now, to truly be a Guiding Light—and not only for a certain part of the population.

Finding resolve in that decision, Uriel mentally prepared himself for his task. One step at a time, just like he'd said—and the first step was to heal the man who needed him so much.

The tiny ship crossed the distance between the compound outskirts and the city in record time. As he stole a look out the window, Uriel caught a glimpse of the agora where the Temple of Genesis rose. They bypassed it so fast that Uriel barely managed to identify the lights from its torches. The aircraft advanced toward the edge of the city, the suburbs where Uriel had never been allowed to go.

In spite of the speed of his transport, Uriel instantly noticed the change. The brightly lit, stone-paved streets Uriel usually traveled through turned into alleys framed by quiet metal buildings. The occasional group of purist guards patrolled the narrow streets, and the black of their uniforms almost made them melt into the general gloom of the area. In the distance, massive buildings loomed, and Uriel wondered how he'd never seen them before. Had he truly been so blind to everything that surrounded him?

The aircraft bypassed the factories and entered a different zone. At last it stopped over a junkyard. Some of the containers marked for cremation moved aside, and the ship slowly glided down, into the underground.

As soon as the aircraft landed, Logan clapped his hands together. "Damn, that was a rush."

Raze exchanged handshakes or hugs with his soldiers. "Mission complete, guys. You did great. This is a huge victory for the resistance, and it could be the chance we've been waiting for."

In spite of the earlier seriousness, the cyborgs seemed to perk up at Raze's words. They patted Raze's back, wishing him luck with his father. Some of them threw uncertain glances Uriel's way, but they didn't address him. They left the ship one by one, until only Logan, Raze, and Uriel remained onboard.

"Well, Guiding Light, ready to go through with your promise?" Logan asked.

Uriel left his seat and nodded. "Always."

"You're very confident. I truly hope it won't be for naught."

Raze glared at his friend, and he probably would have said something biting in Uriel's defense, but another man boarded the ship. He seemed younger than Raze and Logan—likely a few years older than Uriel—but something about him, perhaps his cheekbones or his deep black eyes, reminded Uriel of Raze.

He was not surprised when Raze enthusiastically hugged the new arrival. "This is my brother, Julian. Jules, this is Uriel."

"It's a pleasure to meet you," the other man said—well, he mouthed.

Uriel didn't even blink. As CC-induced afflictions went, muteness wasn't very unusual. Because of the area ID chips had been implanted in, their short-circuiting led to serious afflictions, especially in young children. "The pleasure is all mine," he replied.

"Do you truly think you'll be able to help Father?" Julian inquired, wringing his hands.

"I hope so," Uriel answered. "I have to admit that until recently, I myself didn't think I had much power. But since I met Raze, that's changed. So… I will do my very best."

"Well then, we should get you through the scan and go right ahead with your miracle working," Logan said. "Right this way."

Logan and Julian descended the ramp that led out of the aircraft and entered into a world entirely different from Uriel's. The smell of burned garbage struck Uriel hard, as did the whirring from what seemed to be a million different machines. Sparks of electricity flew around them, landing on the metal floor inches from Uriel. Logan, Raze, and Julian kept walking, not taken aback at all, so Uriel gathered this had to be normal for them. Taking his cues from Raze, Uriel continued on as well.

They entered an elevator, which carried them lower down, deeper into the underground compound. Uriel found it ironic that his own home in the past years had been underground, and yet so impossibly different from this.

As if to confirm Uriel's thoughts, the door of the elevator slid open, revealing a large, busy—and seemingly endless corridor. On each side of the hallway, metal staircases led up to superior floors, where metal doors indicated what Uriel guessed to be various living quarters. The heat emanating from the junkyard's disposing units became even more striking, and Uriel started to have trouble breathing.

Uriel had the urge to ask how anyone could willingly live here, but that would have been rude and snobbish. From the corner of his eye, he caught sight of a female cyborg speaking to a child on one of the upper levels. Both her arms were purely mechanical—which Uriel guessed must mean she'd been a craftsman or a soldier of sorts before the virus. The child appeared to be a regular boy, with a minimal CC that naturally mimicked the genetic changes in his parents' DNA. Still, he didn't seem taken aback when those robotic arms wrapped around him, even if one of her hands wasn't in working order. The child had hurt himself—perhaps playing—so she kissed his palm and pulled him into one of the rooms, for what Uriel guessed would be more scientifically oriented medical care. All the while, the boy kept giggling, like he was having fun in spite of his mother chastising him.

Uriel had never had a mother to hold him, kiss his aches better, and encourage him when things didn't go his way. He'd never played games like children his age and didn't even remember what it was like to genuinely laugh.

He realized then that the luxuries he'd taken for granted all of his life meant nothing. These people benefited from something far more precious, something Uriel would always be denied. Freedom.

He only realized he'd stopped when Raze put his hand on his shoulder. "Hey. Are you all right?"

Uriel turned toward the other man and forced a smile. "Fine. I suppose I'm just a little hot."

Raze winced. "That's understandable. We need to bind your hair back."

Focusing on practicalities helped Uriel snap out of his morose trance. He took in Raze's close-cropped black hair and compared it with his own obscenely long tresses. Yes, most definitely he had to bind it somehow. He should have done so before Raze had arrived at the compound, but he'd been so worried and distracted that it hadn't even occurred to him.

"Come this way," Logan told them. "It'll be cooler in the medical ward."

Uriel quickly complied, noting the disapproving glance Logan shot him. "I've never understood the propensity of some people to sacrifice practicality for fashion," the cyborg needled Uriel. "Why would you even want to have such long hair?"

"It is practical for me," Uriel argued.

Logan scoffed. "I'll bet it is. In your fancy home, you wouldn't have any trouble with too much heat or fuel fumes."

"That's true," Uriel replied, "but it has more to do with the fact that my hair is a tool. During ceremonial days, believers touch it and feel connected to me. If I didn't have it, they'd have to touch my body—and that would be a problem, in more than one way."

Logan rolled his eyes, but Julian pressed a hand to his shoulder while Raze pulled Uriel aside. "Don't let him get to you. He doesn't know you like I do."

"In some ways, he's right," Uriel admitted. "I'm not accustomed to this sort of living."

"I imagine not," Raze answered. "You might not be aware of this, but the virus almost thrust us all into the Dark Ages. The cyborgs who remained in working order were enlisted to fix that—at which point, the factories were created. A lot of the tech is still gone or considered too dangerous by the purists, but we've accepted it more eagerly—which is why we managed to find refuge down here."

It was fascinating to hear Raze speak about his home. Apparently, he'd been the one to organize the resistance, and it had also been his idea to have the headquarters under the junkyard, where the purists would never think of searching or question the high consumption of energy.

Raze's words distracted Uriel, and before he knew it, they reached their destination. Logan guided him into a workshop of sorts and to a scanner that was supposed to detect any tracking devices on Uriel's person. Raze made a move to take over settling the sensors on Uriel's body, but Uriel shook his head. Logan had to do it if the man was ever going to believe he meant well.

In spite of his obvious dislike for Uriel, Logan didn't prolong the arduous process. He didn't even touch Uriel's skin at all. It might not have been for Uriel's benefit, but Uriel was still happy about it.

As Logan settled himself in front of some monitors, Uriel stood there patiently and looked straight at Raze to distract himself from the buzz of the machines. It made him nervous and more than aware of the fluttering in his stomach and his fingertips.

He breathed through it and told himself not to be scared. He had nothing to hide, and he'd come here to help. He couldn't expect the cyborgs to blindly trust his intentions, but perhaps after this, they might stop considering him an enemy.

Logan released some very creative curses, and the sensors on Uriel's body buzzed—not an altogether pleasant sensation. Fortunately, it didn't last for too long, and soon the agitated beeping stopped altogether.

Uriel almost expected something to go wrong, but as it turned out, he needn't have worried. Logan released a soft huff that seemed to convey relief or maybe exasperation. "Well, according to the scanners, you're clear, although…. Some sort of current passed through your body. The voltage wasn't high enough to short-circuit the machine, but it was a close call."

Uriel winced. "Sorry about that. It must have been because of my power."

Logan hummed thoughtfully and started to remove the sensors. He snagged Uriel's hair a single time, but after that, everything went smoothly. "To tell you the truth," he said, "I still don't trust you. But you don't have any tracking devices on you and your presence can help us greatly. So, good luck."

As if in a sign of truce, he passed Uriel a metal hair clip. "Thank you," Uriel said as he pinned his hair back. "I hope I can help."

Now that he'd been given the all clear, it was time for Uriel to show what he was made of. When Uriel and his three companions left the room with the scanner, he found quite a crowd had gathered outside. No one said anything. They just eyed Uriel with clear wariness and distrust. One man in particular glared at him with obvious hatred, but Uriel didn't address it. He looked forward and stuck to Raze's side, hoping that his nervousness wouldn't make him stumble.

The crowd made no move to follow them, but the tension still weighed heavily on Uriel. That didn't change in the slightest when he, Logan, Raze, and Julian entered a medical room outfitted with more tech than Uriel had ever seen in one place. There were monitors that registered a patient's pulse, machines that helped breathing, tubes designed to provide nutrients, and many other wires that Uriel couldn't even identify. They were all connected to a big tube, where a thin old man lay motionless.

Even from the distance, Uriel was struck by the high CC this man must have had at one time. For obvious reasons, the implants no longer worked, but their effects still lingered. Uriel had thought that all the cyborgs with such cybernetic coefficients had been killed by the virus, but apparently he'd been mistaken.

As if reading his mind, Raze proceeded to explain, "My father was a professional soldier before the virus struck. Back then, getting another implant meant an investment for the future. Being stronger and faster could save your life. It was a race between countries and between each soldier in particular. But even before the implants, my father was a very strong man. We think that's the only reason why, against all odds, he survived."

The softly spoken words held so much emotion they brought tears to Uriel's eyes. He and his parents had never had an actual relationship, but Raze obviously worshiped his father. Beyond

90

Uriel's goal to promote cooperation between cyborgs and purists, he wanted to make Raze happy.

Taking a deep breath, Uriel approached the tube. Raze's father seemed to have replaced most of his vital organs with implants that should have made him surpass the limitations of normal humans. The virus had basically shut down those implants, leaving the old man a vegetable.

Upon pressing his fingers over the glass of the cyber tube, Uriel figured out that he couldn't miraculously return Raze's father to his old glory. "If I suddenly reboot all of his implants, his body will never sustain them," he told Raze.

Julian released an inaudible gasp, while Raze's Adam's apple bobbed as he swallowed convulsively. "So you can't help him?"

"I didn't say that," Uriel answered after a small pause. "I can do it gradually—but he is still very weak. We're going to need doctors to watch his vital signs. Understand, I can't guarantee the success of what I'm about to do. It worked on you, but you are young, strong, and healthy."

Logan muttered something that sounded an awful lot like "fraud." Meanwhile, Raze pulled his brother aside. Julian asked his brother something, and Raze hugged him. Because of the size of the room, Uriel heard Raze reply, "I trust Uriel, and right now, he's the only chance we have."

The weight of Raze's belief in him settled over Uriel like a comforting veil. His family's expectations had always been a burden, but not so in Raze's case. He didn't know why, but Raze's presence and his faith empowered Uriel, made him feel like he was more than an empty object of so-called worship, that he could actually do something with his life.

Raze and Julian turned toward him, and both nodded. "Do your thing. Julian and I are the ones who've always cared for our father. If something happens, we'll be watching."

Uriel turned away from Raze and focused on the tube and the man inside it. It would have been ideal if he'd been able to come into contact with the man's skin, but perhaps it was better this way. Having a barrier between them might keep Uriel's power from striking Raze's father too hard.

At first nothing happened. Uriel attempted to reach out to that part of him that had responded to the implants of every single believer and had helped Raze, but it refused to comply. His power shied away from the injured man, acknowledging what Uriel would have noticed even without Raze telling him—the looming touch of death.

Uriel gritted his teeth and recalled Raze's words, pulling them to the forefront of his mind. He remembered the image of the cyborg woman with her child and that of Julian's dismayed eyes. He could do this. He had to.

Power burst out of him and toward the comatose cyborg. Uriel quickly reeled it in before it could lash out against his patient. Somewhere deep inside, he found an anchor in how much he wanted to give Raze his father back. He used that need to reach out to the sick man, slowly insinuating himself into the cyborg's body.

The moment he connected with his patient, pain erupted over him. It wasn't a physical pain that Uriel could have easily understood. Rather, it felt like... being disconnected, torn away from reality and thrust into a dark void of nothingness. Needles seemed to pierce every inch of Uriel's body, and his lungs filled with liquid, rendering him unable to breathe. All the while, that darkness battered Uriel's mind, nearly driving him into oblivion.

Bits and pieces of incoherent memories lunged at him like daggers, exploding within Uriel's consciousness. Uriel tried to remain focused, but his attempts failed spectacularly when he found himself propelled into one particularly potent recollection.

A small dark-haired boy suddenly stood in front of him, staring up at him with wide, painfully familiar eyes. "Daddy, what happened? Where's Mommy?"

"Mommy is in heaven now, son," Uriel—or rather Raze's father, whose memories Uriel now inhabited—said. "But she'll always be watching over us. Always."

"What's... heaven?" the child inquired.

"It's a beautiful place, one where all good people go after the world becomes too difficult for them. God made it for us."

"People say there is no God," the boy answered, his voice trembling. "What happened, Daddy? Where did she go?"

Raze's father hugged his son, shushing his cries. "God is always there, watching, even if people don't believe. Your mother was very sick, but she is with him now."

"But the doctors...." The child's lower lip trembled as he spoke. "They said they would help her."

"And they tried, Raze, but sometimes bad things happen. Your mother did leave us with one last beautiful gift. You have a little brother now. His name is Julian."

The image of a tiny, scrunched-up baby appeared in Uriel's mind's eye. "You're going to have to be brave, little man. Julian is going to need you, and he'll need me. It's just the three of us now, Raze."

The memory faded, and in its place, a man appeared. He looked like an older version of Raze: tall, muscular, with those same piercing black eyes that enchanted Uriel. It was very hard for Uriel to reconcile this image with the crippled old man in the tube, but he still identified the stranger as Raze's father.

"What is this?" the man asked. "Who are you?"

"My name is Uriel. I'm a friend of your sons. You were sick for a very long time."

"Sick?" The man arched a brow. "Permit me to doubt that. Given my CC, I'm immune to most if not all diseases."

"Yes, but...." Uriel hesitated, not sure how to explain the situation. "There was a virus. It hit every single implant, from simple ID chips to body improvements. People with high CCs were struck hardest."

"You must be joking." Raze's father scowled. "That couldn't possibly happen. It doesn't make any logical sense. No virus would be able to cause such destruction. They weren't built in a network that would allow the propagation of a virus."

Uriel had heard many theories about the root causes of the virus—none of which had found a satisfactory explanation. "I know it seems shocking," he said quietly, "but it's true."

Something in Uriel's tone must have convinced Raze's father of the truth of his words. All the blood drained from the other man's face, making him look a little more like his real-life image. "That can't be," he whispered. "No…. My sons? What happened to Raze? Julian?"

"They're all right," Uriel rushed to assure the cyborg. "Their implants did suffer, but they're alive."

He didn't think it was a good time to mention Julian's muteness, so instead, he explained, "I have certain abilities that allow me to make implants work again. Raze came to me so that I'd help you recover."

"I have no idea who you are, young man, or if you're even telling the truth," the cyborg replied, "but it's obvious that something happened to me if I'm even in this condition in the first place. So let's start at the beginning. I'm Lucius Hartman. What's your name, and how did you get in my head?"

Chapter Six

RAZE HELD his breath as he watched Uriel attempt the impossible. He told himself not to hope for too much, but at the same time, something inside him screamed that Uriel could and would do this.

At first Uriel closed his eyes and became almost abnormally still. A few minutes passed while nothing happened. Then his body went rigid, and he released a small, barely audible gasp. He swayed, and Raze rushed to his side, catching Uriel before the other man could fall.

He was very careful not to touch Uriel's skin, because the results would have probably been quite disastrous. Already, a slight current of energy was passing through Uriel, and Raze feared that any moment now, he'd be knocked out by the bioenergy.

It didn't happen. Uriel seemed completely focused on Raze's father. Lucius's pulse began to spike, and Julian quickly approached, hovering over the monitors as he got ready to intervene should the worst come to pass.

In Raze's arms, Uriel started to seize. He was making low whimpering noises that just about broke Raze's heart. Finally, his body went limp. Well no, that wasn't exactly accurate. He did lean against Raze, as if by instinct, but at the same time, his hand stuck to the cyber tube, not moving even when Uriel seemed no longer able to support himself on his own two feet.

Raze didn't know what to look at. He occasionally stole glimpses at the machine and at his father's face but then quickly focused on Uriel. For the first time, it occurred to him that he'd asked a great deal of the younger man. Uriel himself had admitted to not being very experienced with using his power, and Raze had thrust him into healing a man who hovered at the edge of death. If only he'd thought to go see the Guiding Light sooner. If something happened to either his father or Uriel, it would be solely Raze's fault.

When Uriel went deathly silent, Raze didn't know if he should be frightened or relieved. Uriel's body had now gone as taut as a bowstring, but he kept twitching rhythmically. At one point, Raze realized that each of the twitches followed the rhythm of his father's heartbeat. Raze wasn't sure if he should consider that encouraging or not.

He went for "not" when the machines monitoring his father's condition started beeping alarmingly. In Raze's arms, Uriel began to writhe, his hand like a claw on the cyber tube.

Logan cursed, rushing to Julian's assistance as Raze's brother struggled to stabilize their father's condition. Raze would have liked to help too, but at the same time, he couldn't bring himself to let go of Uriel. His head spun, his heart raced, and he'd never felt more helpless in his life.

At last the beeping of the monitors settled down, and Raze's father took a deep breath. He didn't open his eyes, not right then, but Raze realized what was happening nonetheless.

"Shit," Logan said, confirming Raze's suspicions, "his implants are starting to work."

Julian shot Raze a look full of uncertain hope, and Raze forced a smile for his brother's benefit. "Take him off the artificial breathing," he told Julian. "Quickly. It's just hindering him now."

Julian complied, and Raze waited to see the reaction. Nothing really happened. His father kept breathing on his own, like he'd never stopped, like Raze hadn't spent hours staring at the machines that kept his lungs from completely collapsing.

Uriel, on the other hand, seemed to be having trouble breathing. In spite of the fact that it had been bound back, his long hair had gone sweaty, curling over his nape. Raze dared to touch him, placing his hand over Uriel's on the tube. He found it cold and clammy.

Meanwhile, Logan and Julian kept their eyes focused on Raze's father. "It's working," Logan said. "It's actually working. Don't let him move away, Raze. He's doing it."

Raze bristled when he realized that his friend and his brother didn't care in the slightest about what happened to Uriel. In a way, he understood it, and perhaps he had his priorities all wrong. After all, his father should have been more important than a man he'd met a few days ago.

Even so, right then and there, Raze wanted nothing more than to pull Uriel's hand away. That urge became more powerful when Uriel started making alarming gurgling noises. Raze struggled to remain calm, but inside he was screaming. He made sure Uriel's mouth was open and supported the younger man's head as Uriel threw up. And still, even as Uriel emptied the contents of his stomach, he didn't release his hold on the cyber tube. It was like something beyond his physical abilities kept him bound to it.

After making sure Uriel's mouth was clear and no risk existed of him inhaling his own vomit, Raze tried to set Uriel down, naturally avoiding the puddle. The angle made it nearly impossible. When Raze physically tried to pull Uriel's hand away from the tube, it wouldn't budge. He tried again and again, but the only time he managed to lift one of Uriel's fingers, the machines began to beep again, and a current shot through his body, nearly shutting Raze's mental computer down. Okay, he'd gotten the message.

Stumped, Raze held Uriel in his arms, supporting him as best he could. It seemed that with every implant Uriel was fixing, his own body absorbed the aftereffects of that particular organ's failure. Raze could only hope this would be temporary.

The scent of urine reached Raze's nostrils, and Raze really wanted to cry. He reached out to his mental computer, trying to assess his possible courses of action. "If you attempt to stop the process before it is completed," the computer warned him, "the energy that is fixing the implants will recoil against the parties involved. It could kill them both."

Raze had suspected that much. Feeling like he carried the weight of the world on his shoulders, he started whispering soft endearments in Uriel's ear. He himself didn't know what he said. The words were a blur, lost in the turmoil of his emotions. He could see that with every torturous second that passed, his father's condition improved. Already Lucius had regained some of his color. But in his heart, Raze couldn't help but wonder if the price to be paid would be too high.

After what seemed like forever, the torture stopped. With a soft sigh, Uriel went still in Raze's arms. His hand dropped from where it had remained glued to the cyber tube. Dread rose inside Raze, and for a single horrible moment, he feared the worst while praying for Uriel to recover and come back to him. Maybe someone up there did hear him, because Uriel slowly cracked his eyes open, blinking several times as he struggled to focus. "Raze…. Did it work?"

Raze threw a look toward his father, just in time to see the man stir to consciousness.

"Raze, is that you?" he asked, his voice rusty from disuse.

Raze had been waiting for this moment for years. He'd almost lost all hope—until he'd met Uriel. And now, when he could finally speak to his father again, his heart was heavy because of the pain he'd watched Uriel suffer through.

Swallowing around the sudden knot in his throat, Raze nodded. "It's me, Father. How do you feel?"

The top of the cyber tube slid open, and Raze's father rubbed his eyes, groaning. "Weaker than I ever remember being." He looked around the room, frowning. "Where's Julian? Your friend said nothing had happened to him."

Julian stepped into their father's line of sight and waved. The older man's eyes widened. "How long was I unconscious?" he asked. "Julian…. You're all grown up."

"It's been twenty years, Father," Raze answered—because his brother couldn't. A part of him wanted to embrace the man he'd worshiped for the better part of his life. But his priorities had changed somewhere along the way, because right now, Raze could only think about caring for the brave young man in his arms.

Thankfully, Julian had already shot into action, proceeding to check their father's vitals and to make sure the miraculous recovery wasn't a fluke. Logan approached Raze and patted him on the shoulder. "Good job, Raze," he said. "I didn't think you had it in you to push him—"

"Stop," Raze said, interrupting his friend. "Stop before you say something that'll make me punch you."

Raze had always cared for his friend deeply, and Logan had been there for him through thick and thin. But Raze had never seen him act so deliberately callous before. Hell, Logan seemed to think that Raze had maintained his hold on Uriel to force the healing process to continue despite the difficulties Uriel was having. It nauseated Raze that Logan considered such an action justified.

He'd never realized this simple fact about himself or any of his fellow members of the resistance. They could be as cruel and self-righteous as the purists. Raze was the first to rejoice because of his father's recovery, but that didn't lessen his pain over what Uriel had been forced to endure. Uriel seemed to have surpassed the episode that had gripped him, because both his breathing and his heart rate had evened to normality. That didn't make Raze any less angry on his behalf.

Oddly enough, it was his father who stopped any possible argument. "It looks like you've grown up too, son," he said. When Raze looked at him, he found the other man smiling.

"You've found something, or rather someone, to protect. I'm so happy I got to see it."

Raze acknowledged his father's words with a nod. He wanted to say more, but he realized he didn't have to. If there was anyone who understood, it was his father. The man had loved Raze's mother with absolute devotion, and he'd been crushed when she died. He'd seen and grasped what Uriel meant to Raze.

"Julian, take care of Father, would you? Let me know if anything happens. I have to go see to Uriel."

Julian nodded, his eyes very wide as he finally took in Uriel's curled-up form. Uriel said nothing, simply hiding behind the fall of his now-loose long hair and clutching Raze's shoulder with a trembling hand. Following his instincts, Raze nodded a silent "thank you" to his father and turned on his heel. As he carried his precious bundle out of the room, however, he ran straight into a swarm of cyborgs.

One thing about his people—they could be very determined, and they used what gifts they had left with almost ruthless skill. It didn't surprise Raze that they had already figured out Uriel had succeeded in his attempt to heal Raze's father. Few people here had known Lucius Hartman in his glory days, but that didn't matter. Simply overhearing the brief conversation between Raze and his father had been enough.

And so Raze—or rather Uriel—suddenly became the focus of the entire resistance in a very different way. Men and women mobbed them, blocking Raze's path and trying to address Uriel.

"My sister had an implant that improved her memory and learning capacity. After the virus, she can't even remember her own name. Maybe... you could try to help her."

"My husband can't move his legs since the virus. It's been such a struggle because he was always such an active man. Please, won't you heal him?"

"My brother's eye implants blinded him when the virus struck. Help him. I'm sure you can do it."

Request after request flew Uriel's way. Uriel shied away from them, burying his face in Raze's chest like a child. When someone actually reached for Uriel, Raze snarled, "Back off. He's in no condition to help anyone right now."

He didn't even wait for a reply. Instead, he pushed through the gathered crowd, feeling a small measure of satisfaction when the other cyborgs hastily moved out of his way.

They reached Raze's quarters in record time. The moment the door closed behind them, Raze punched in his security code, ensuring that they wouldn't be disturbed. He carried Uriel to the small bathing facility adjoining his room. Down here and among the cyborgs, running water was a precious commodity. Julian had set up an alternative to be used for cleaning purposes—a pressure steam shower that cleansed the body using the loose hydrogen and oxygen atoms. It didn't have the same feel as a real water shower like the purists used, but it was definitely effective.

He carried Uriel into the shower and placed him on the small bench. As Raze punched in the command for the cleansing module, Uriel watched him quietly, as if not knowing what to make of his actions. If Raze had to guess, Uriel had probably never seen a pressure shower before. He decided to explain, because otherwise, his actions might scare Uriel.

Kneeling in front of Uriel, he gazed into his charge's green eyes. "I'm going to help you out of your clothes now, okay, Uriel? I'll give you a shower, and then you can get some rest. How does that sound?"

"A s-shower?" Uriel stammered, paling. "In here?"

Raze nodded. "We don't use running water. It's probably nothing like what you're used to, but I assure you, it's safe. I'll be here, and I won't—"

Before Raze could even finish the phrase, Uriel shot to his feet and pushed him away. "Thank you for your offer, but that won't be necessary," he blurted out with striking formality. "I can handle this on my own."

Raze might have been inclined to respect Uriel's decision, except the younger man swayed, obviously still weak from his ordeal. He caught Uriel's arm, keeping him from falling. "I know it's hard for you to accept the touch of others, but—"

Yet again, Uriel interrupted him. "That's not it. I don't mind it when it's you."

In spite of the less than ideal circumstances, Raze's dick twitched in his pants. Raze leashed his libido and focused on the man in front of him. "Then what is it, baby?" he asked. "What are you afraid of?"

"You shouldn't see me like this," Uriel said, not meeting his eyes. "I'm not pure."

Not pure? Shit. It hadn't even occurred to Raze that Uriel might be embarrassed by losing control of his most basic functions. "Oh, Uriel…. Look at me. Come on, look at me." When Uriel hesitantly lifted his eyes, Raze dared to brush his fingers over Uriel's cheek. "You and I are very different, as different as night and day. For many years, I considered you my foe—even at a time when you were too young to understand what was happening. I'm not proud of that. I realize now it was a mistake. Because four days ago, when we met…. Seeing you, holding you, trusting you—it changed my life. You are the purest, bravest, and kindest person I've ever met, and not because you're the Guiding Light, but because you're you. So let me take care of you, just this once. You're not alone anymore."

He wanted to say more, but he was already rambling, and he didn't want to scare Uriel more than he already had. He helped Uriel sit down again, petting his hair softly.

Uriel bit his lower lip, seemingly musing over Raze's words. "You won't think ill of me?" he asked at last, hesitantly reaching for Raze's hand.

"Never." It was a promise he could truly make without fear of failure. He'd been unable to protect Uriel so far, but he wouldn't allow distrust to grip him again.

After a few seconds of vacillation, Uriel took a deep breath and nodded. "All right. As long as you're not disgusted."

Raze didn't even address that comment with words. Instead, he gripped Uriel's boot and slowly pulled it off. Uriel winced, and Raze noticed the reason when he fully removed the footwear. Shockingly, they had chafed Uriel's feet.

Raze wanted to kick himself. He'd been wearing this type of boot for years, and he'd never had any sort of discomfort. But Uriel wasn't used to them. As the Guiding Light, he wore loose robes and sandals, and in spite of his great power, he clearly remained delicate in some regards. Why hadn't Raze realized it? God, he was such an idiot.

Uriel seemed to notice Raze's anger with himself and perhaps misinterpreted it, because he pulled his foot from Raze's grip. "I'm sorry. It'll heal quickly, I promise. It's nothing."

Raze mentally counted to ten and reined in his temper—even if it drove him crazy that Uriel considered it necessary to apologize for getting hurt. "How do you know?" he asked as he reached for the other boot.

His casual, cautious demeanor turned out to be the right choice, because Uriel relaxed. "I'm trained for it," he explained. "During ceremonial days, we use certain substances that keep me from sweating, feeling lust, needing to rest or do my private needs. After that, I get all sorts of injuries, but it's fine. They pass."

Raze had seen bits and pieces of Uriel's memories, enough to know that Uriel had been trapped inside the gilded cage of his compound. He'd also caught glimpses of Uriel injured, but he'd never made the full connection with the ceremonial days. What Uriel was saying sounded horrible, because suppressing the natural functioning of the human kidneys or perspiratory glands could be very dangerous.

Uriel didn't seem concerned, and he also took the injuries to his feet in stride. In fact, Raze suspected that any moment now, Uriel would change his mind and decide to push him away after all.

And so Raze buried his hatred for the purists deep inside and melted it into the desire to lavish Uriel with affection. He didn't speak, but he did press small kisses over the injuries on Uriel's legs. To Raze's surprise, Uriel twitched a little, but this time it wasn't an action caused by pain. He was ticklish.

Raze filed that little tidbit away for later use and went on to remove Uriel's top. It had largely managed to avoid being splattered with vomit, but it would need washing too. Raze tossed it in the laundry compartment and made a mental note to provide Uriel with a different outfit, hopefully a more comfortable one.

When he reached Uriel's pants, the younger man tensed. As if on cue, Uriel said, "Maybe I should…."

Raze looked up at Uriel and waited. He wanted to do this for Uriel, to show him that sometimes it was okay to be vulnerable and that he didn't always have to be the strong one whom everybody relied on. Besides, Uriel might be pretending he was all right, but he would have never agreed to Raze assisting him if he'd completely recovered from his fit.

As Uriel trailed off, Raze began to undo the bindings of the other man's trousers. Uriel winced, studiously looking away, but didn't protest again. He did shimmy his ass, helping Raze pull off his pants but still biting his lower lip in that distinctive display of uncertainty that both angered Raze and made him want to kiss the breath out of Uriel. He followed his instincts and very carefully pushed the material down, not reacting in the slightest when he found it still moist. Once Uriel was naked, Raze punched in the final command that would start the shower. He didn't take off his own clothes, because the implications of such an action would be something Uriel didn't need right then and there.

Uriel gasped slightly when the shower cabin filled with mist. As the minute particles of hydrogen and oxygen assaulted Uriel's body, his eyes widened comically, like he didn't know what to make of the alien sensation.

Smiling, Raze returned to Uriel's side and reached for the soap dispenser. He squirted a generous amount of the clear liquid in his palm and gestured for Uriel to turn around. "Relax," he told Uriel. "Close your eyes and don't think about anything."

It was far easier said than done—not thinking didn't come naturally to human beings, especially not to Uriel, who seemed predisposed to shoulder the brunt of burdens he shouldn't have to carry. Still, Uriel gave it a shot, perhaps for Raze's sake. He closed his eyes and changed his position, giving Raze access to his long, flowing locks. His heart hammering, Raze focused on fulfilling his promise, on dispersing Uriel's fears and doubts, not through his words but through his actions.

With nearly excruciating care, he lathered the soapy liquid in Uriel's hair and massaged Uriel's scalp, all the while testing Uriel's reactions for an increase in tension. It didn't happen. Uriel actually released a soft sigh of pleasure that went straight to Raze's cock. Gritting his teeth, Raze focused on finding the areas that had triggered that response in Uriel.

He ignored the demands of his own body, because Uriel was the one who mattered now. He kept each touch affectionate but platonic, and he was rewarded when Uriel melted against him, completely boneless.

Uriel's hair felt like silk between his fingers. Now moist because of the steam, it fell heavily past Uriel's shoulders, drawing the eye to the elegant curve of Uriel's back. Reaching every lock of hair turned out to be quite a problematic task but one Raze accepted and delved into with more than a little enjoyment.

When he was satisfied that his massage had relaxed Uriel, Raze proceeded to soap up the younger man's shoulders. He expected Uriel to tense—touching skin was different from touching hair—but Uriel leaned into his caress, like a cat craving the affection of the human who pretended to be his master.

The way he flipped his hair with unconscious sensuality had Raze in dumbstruck awe. Even if it was an inappropriate moment to consider something sexual, Raze wanted to see more of Uriel. His own lusts aside, this moment was precious because Uriel had opened himself up to him in a way he wouldn't have with anyone else.

Raze traced the lines of Uriel's shoulders with his thumbs, finding the spots that held the most accumulated tension. He focused

Enetn欸

on those areas, drawing a moan out of Uriel. The young man literally slumped against him, which made it hard for Raze to continue the process.

On the other hand, Raze couldn't bring himself to protest the near embrace. Having Uriel in his arms always felt so right. It also reminded him of the last time he'd carried Uriel—when Uriel had struggled through such a painful process while healing Raze's father. He mentally chastised himself for allowing Uriel to become an object of his lust, when Uriel needed something else entirely.

From that point on, Raze suppressed his natural draw toward Uriel. He'd expected it to be hard, and in a sense it was, obscenely so. However, with each moment that passed, something else grew inside him, his need to protect Uriel more important than any other goal or desire he'd ever had. He swept his hands over Uriel's body with gentle care, cleaning his torso then progressing lower down to his abdomen. With great reluctance, he freed Uriel from his embrace and supported him against the shower wall. Kneeling in front of him once more, he proceeded to wash Uriel's legs and his still wounded feet.

He left the most delicate area, Uriel's crotch, for last. He knew all too well that it was likely to make Uriel uncomfortable. Sure, just the sight of that slender shaft and the perfect spheres of Uriel's testicles tested Raze's resolve. Fuck, those pretty, plump balls were made for Raze's mouth. But Raze was nothing if not persistent, and when he reached for Uriel's dick his hand didn't tremble and his touch remained no-nonsense—one friend helping another in his time of need and nothing more.

He thought he'd succeeded in the impossible, but then a smothered sniff drew his attention. Raze looked up, only to be greeted by the sight of Uriel's tearstained face.

"What is it, Uriel?" he asked, alarmed. "Did I hurt you?"

Uriel shook his head, but his tears kept flowing. "It's nothing. I just... I'm being stupid."

Raze brushed his fingers over Uriel's cheeks, wiping away the crystalline drops of liquid. "Won't you tell me, baby?"

RAZE'S GENTLENESS almost broke Uriel's heart. He didn't know how to explain his own feelings, since they baffled and confused him. For as long as he could remember, he'd suffered the aftereffects of ceremonial days alone, where no one could see him and realize he wasn't as perfect as they all wanted him to be.

But Raze had seen him at his worst and wasn't disgusted with him. Raze treated him with more kindness than Uriel had ever experienced in his entire life. Raze called him 'baby,' and the word held genuine affection. But Uriel guessed it to be solely because of gratitude. Raze might have liked him up to this point, but he hadn't seen Uriel's weak side. Not to mention that, no matter how much Uriel would have liked to pretend, Raze didn't and would never belong to him.

"Baby?" Raze prodded, his dark eyes scrutinizing Uriel's face in obvious anxiousness. "Talk to me. Are you all right?"

There it was, that pet name again. It made Uriel ache for things that couldn't be. He shook himself, feeling stupid and ridiculous for allowing his emotions to run amok this way. "I'm fine. Just a little shaken."

Raze narrowed his eyes, not seeming convinced by Uriel's bravado. Nonetheless, he didn't confront Uriel with his obvious lie. "All right. Let's finish up here, and then you can get some rest. You'll feel better in no time."

Uriel had to say something, anything. He didn't want Raze to believe that Uriel was wary of his touch, like he'd been with Logan. When Raze made a move to pull away, Uriel went with his instincts—or perhaps with his panic—and grabbed the other man's arm. "Stay with me," he whispered.

It might have been a selfish thing to say. It might have even been inadequate for the Guiding Light. But Uriel was tired of living by the arbitrary standards others had set. Just this once, he'd allow himself to take the comfort Raze offered. It would only hurt more once he and Raze parted ways, but for now, Uriel wouldn't think about that.

Raze didn't answer, at least not through words. He did, however, return to Uriel's side. He met Uriel's gaze, and his hands swept over Uriel's skin. Using the gathered moisture in the air, he continued to wash Uriel with the same gentleness as before, like nothing had happened.

And in spite of that very same moisture, Uriel's tears dried. His body trembled, but it was no longer because of the weakness lingering from his efforts to heal Lucius Hartman. Suddenly he could see past his own feelings of self-pity and embarrassment, and he realized how much he wanted Raze to hold him, just like Raze had before. He couldn't bring himself to fear getting addicted to it, because that ship had already sailed.

As if guessing his thoughts, Raze pulled him close and kissed his forehead. Instinctively, Uriel pressed himself to Raze's side. When Raze was with him, it felt like they'd known each other forever. In spite of all the uncertainties, Uriel could truly believe he'd made the right choices today.

He forced himself to face Raze, scanning the other man's face, wondering what Raze thought about all this. Raze's dark locks had gone moist in the pressure shower, and for some reason the sight of them hypnotized Uriel. Unable to help himself, he reached out and clutched what little he could of Raze's close-cropped hair.

"Uriel...." Raze whispered, and the sound of his name on Raze's lips somehow made Uriel shiver.

"You're different," Uriel blurted out. "When everyone else tries to touch me, I feel so violated, like they're forcing themselves on me. But when it's you... it's so different."

Raze didn't answer. In quick, efficient motions he finished washing Uriel. He even washed Uriel's genitals and his ass, miraculously managing to remain platonic about it. Uriel ached to return the favor—and if he wanted to be perfectly honest, it was largely because he wanted to see Raze naked and to touch Raze *that way*. His face flamed at the thought, but he didn't get the chance to go through with his plan. Raze picked him up and punched in a few more commands. The air in the shower shifted into a pleasant breeze that soon dried both Uriel's hair and his body.

Truly, Uriel's hair was far too thick to completely be rid of moisture, but Raze obviously lost his patience and stepped out of the shower. He placed Uriel onto the one-person cot that filled most of the tiny room and covered him with a thick blanket.

"Get some sleep. I'll go find you some clothes and I'll be right back. Do you think you'll be okay?"

Uriel wanted to tell him to stay, but he didn't. He'd already done so once, and he didn't want to push it. And so he forced a smile and nodded. "I told you I snap back quickly."

Raze didn't seem awfully convinced. He gave Uriel a concerned glance and kissed his forehead once more. "I'll be right back," he repeated. "Rest. You're safe."

With that, Raze turned away from the bed, and after throwing Uriel one last uncertain look, he left the room. As the door slid closed, Uriel's façade of bravery dropped. He curled into the blanket and tried to follow Raze's suggestion, but he simply couldn't do it.

The quilt might have covered him and kept him warm, but he still started to tremble. He didn't remember ever being this needy, clingy person, and he hated himself for it, but now that Raze had left.... He didn't even know what it meant, what would happen.

A new shiver swept through him as he recalled all the people out there, everyone who had seen him and known what he was, what he'd done and how weak he'd been. Without Raze to protect him, he couldn't face them again. Without Raze there, everything rushed back, and he was horrified upon realizing what he'd allowed Raze to see.

And then he recalled Raze's father, all the pain and the memories the older cyborg had kept buried, just so he could make the world better and safer for his two sons. He wanted to cry, but instead he froze, his muscles refusing to obey him as he drifted away into the memories of a man he hadn't known until today. Much to his dismay, he fixed onto the last recollection he'd caught—the very distant one of the moment when Lucius's implants had short-circuited.

He couldn't understand why that particular moment mattered to him, why Lucius's pain suddenly felt like his own. It had been so brief that it barely registered in Lucius's consciousness at all, but for Uriel, it seemed inescapable. By rights, Uriel should have worried about completely different things. But he couldn't let go, couldn't free himself of the fear that threatened to swallow him whole.

He didn't know how much time passed until Raze finally returned. It could have been a few minutes or it could have been an age—but it definitely felt like the latter. When he heard the door slide open, Uriel managed to snap out of his trance but couldn't for the life of him utter a single word. Thankfully, Raze figured out something was wrong. He dropped the clothing he carried on a nearby chair, ran to Uriel, and sat next to him on the bed. "Uriel? Uriel, can you hear me?"

Uriel couldn't make his vocal cords work, and as much as he would have liked to reply, he found himself unable to. Cursing viciously, Raze shoved away the quilt and started rubbing his hands up and down Uriel's arms. He slid next to Uriel and held him close, whispering soft endearments in his ear.

Raze's warmth chased away the panic, and slowly, Uriel regained his ability to breathe. He clutched the material of Raze's shirt, finding refuge in the familiarity of the other man's scent. It was so strange to remember how Raze used to be before the virus had torn his life asunder, but it just drew Uriel to him even more.

Raze caressed his hair, his hand big and strong and strikingly comforting. "Better now?" he asked.

Uriel nodded. Raze's presence made the memories friendlier, pushing him past horrible times to focus on beautiful ones, moments of father and son bonding. "Thank you," he replied. "I'm—"

"Don't you dare say you're sorry," Raze interrupted him. "You saved my father's life today, and it took a lot out of you. That's understandable. I shouldn't have left you alone to begin with."

Technically speaking, Uriel had been the one to reassure Raze, so it had been his mistake, not Raze's. And maybe he'd have said that, but it suddenly dawned on him that he was completely naked. And while Uriel had long ago stopped being particularly shy about his nudity, he'd never been in this position before, so close to someone when he didn't have any clothes on. The only barrier between him and Raze was Raze's clothing, but its tightness guaranteed that Uriel could feel every strong muscle behind the material.

As if of their own accord, Uriel's hands slid under Raze's vest, somehow managing to find their way underneath the garment. Electricity shot through him as he traced the lines of Raze's abdomen with his fingers. Raze obviously felt it too, because he released a tortured groan. "Uriel.... Baby, you shouldn't.... We shouldn't do this."

Uriel didn't even know what "this" was. His experience of real-life contact with anyone was limited to say the least, and if he tried to think too much about it, he would lose his nerve—or his madness, whatever it was that made him reach for Raze. He could only be sure of one thing. He craved to feel Raze against him, like he'd dreamed mere hours ago when he'd allowed himself to masturbate over the other man. He wished he could tell Raze that, but he didn't think he could speak.

With a frustrated huff, Uriel pulled on Raze's vest, trying to push it out of the way. As much as he liked the way the garments clung to Raze's body, right now they were an obstacle to his goal. How in the world had Raze managed to free him from his clothing before? All the buttons and zippers seemed designed to thwart Uriel's less-than-organized efforts.

In his defense, Raze wasn't exactly being cooperative. At first he just lay there, as if afraid what reaction his moving would trigger inside Uriel. In the end, when Uriel's free hand dared to snake

111

toward Raze's crotch—with no input from Raze at all, of course—he must have decided to chance it. Raze grabbed Uriel's hands and stopped him from his tentative assault.

He pinned Uriel to the bed and rolled on top of him, immobilizing him with his larger bulk. His weight felt so good on top of Uriel that he forgot about the lingering shyness that had kept him from speaking. "Touch me," he managed to say. "Please."

Raze's breath caught. "Uriel…. You don't know what you're saying."

Uriel nodded, then shook his head, then slumped onto the small cot, breathless. "I do," he answered, knowing he didn't sound very convincing but unable to help himself. "I want this. All my life, everyone else made decisions in my stead. This time it's my decision. So please…. Touch me."

Of course, Uriel's little speech wasn't in the least bit coherent. Each word—no, each syllable—came out punctuated by a gasp. If he stuttered once or twice…. Well, who could have blamed him?

Not that it mattered. Raze understood, and he stopped protesting. He gazed deeply into Uriel's eyes, as if seeking confirmation of Uriel's words. What he found must have convinced him, because the next thing Uriel knew, Raze's lips landed on his—and it was pure heaven.

Chapter Seven

IT WAS pure heaven. Raze didn't consider himself all that devout, but right now he could certainly believe that a greater power existed—because he couldn't otherwise explain these beautiful moments or the fact that he even had Uriel in his arms.

Uriel's lips felt so soft under his, perfectly plump and full, parting obediently to grant him entrance. Their delightful owner released a low moan, which Raze muffled as he thrust his tongue into the mouth that had been his obsession for what seemed like forever. Uriel responded to the kiss with a great deal of enthusiasm, if not a lot of experience. He ground against Raze frantically, his hard naked dick nudging Raze's clothed one.

It would have taken a man far stronger than Raze to resist the unspoken invitation. Still holding onto Uriel's wrists with one hand, he insinuated the other between their bodies and gripped his soon-to-be lover's dick.

Hot and hard, the shaft twitched in Raze's fist, already leaking copious amounts of precum. Uriel arched against him, releasing a small whimpering noise that went to Raze's head like a shot of electricity. Then again, Uriel's mere presence electrified Raze, short-circuiting his rational side that tried to tell him... something. Maybe.

Whatever Raze's mental computer wanted to say, it would have to wait. Raze tuned it out, foregoing everything except Uriel's beauty. He literally drank in Uriel's cries, unable to tear his mouth away from the other man's even to breathe. After all, who the hell needed oxygen? Uriel's passion was a more than adequate replacement, and kissing Uriel for the rest of his life sounded like a great idea.

He changed his mind when Uriel started to writhe against him, straining against his hold. Uriel couldn't physically free himself from Raze's grip, but the sparks now freely emanating from Uriel's body made every inch of Raze's skin buzz with sexual desire. The energy almost seemed like an extension of Uriel's will, teasing Raze's nipples and pooling into Raze's cock, perhaps because Uriel couldn't touch those parts of Raze with his hands.

Just the same, Uriel did a good job of convincing Raze to move things along. Uriel seemed quite displeased with Raze's still-clothed state, and Raze himself didn't know why in the world he'd kept his garments on up to this point. He must have had a reason—he never did anything without a reason—but right now, he couldn't remember.

Well, he had the perfect solution for it. He broke away from Uriel and in a few angry jerks, removed his vest. His boots were a bit more of a challenge, and by the time he managed to throw them off he was panting, already aching to touch Uriel again. He was struggling with the zipper of his pants—and damn it, the stupid thing had to choose this exact moment to be uncooperative—when Uriel reached for him.

All naked skin and slick muscle, Uriel climbed into Raze's lap. He pressed his mouth to Raze's, his tight ass grinding against Raze's crotch. It was by no means a particularly adventurous kiss, but it held so much promise and yearning that for the first time in memory, Raze came in his pants. He literally came. In. His. Pants.

Uriel must have felt it—not that it was too difficult—because he broke their lip-lock, his eyes wide. Embarrassment heated Raze's face. Ejaculating prematurely had never been a problem for him.

Besides, he wasn't a teenager anymore, and his lack of self-control could really throw a wrench in his plans.

Maybe he would have apologized, but Uriel blushed brightly, all the way to the tips of his ears. He climbed off Raze, mumbling something barely understandable under his breath. Moving on autopilot, Raze managed to take off his pants, peeling the now sticky garment off. Even if they didn't do anything else tonight, he wanted to feel Uriel's naked limbs entwined with his.

And then Uriel did something completely unexpected. Biting his lower lip yet again, he passed a tentative finger through the lingering drops of cum in Raze's pubic hair. When Uriel brought his slender finger to his mouth and sucked it in, Raze's libido flared back to life. In mere seconds, his cock went from half-erect—it could never be completely soft around Uriel—to hard-enough-to-crush-diamonds. Uriel froze with his finger still in his mouth, his lips prettily stretched around it and giving Raze visions of what else Uriel could suck.

As if reading Raze's mind, Uriel glanced from Raze's face to his cock, then back to his face. When he finally released his digit, he brought it down to rub over the head of Raze's dick, prodding at the slit, first hesitantly, then with a little more daring. When Raze let out an encouraging groan, Uriel engulfed Raze's dick in his fist, all the while licking his lips in an unconsciously sensuous gesture.

Raze couldn't take it anymore. He needed to fuck that pretty mouth so badly he ached. Gripping Uriel's long hair, he guided the younger man's head down with far more force than he'd have liked. Because of their positions and the narrow space on the bed, it couldn't have been very comfortable for Uriel, but Uriel didn't seem to mind. In fact, he went with it, arching his back beautifully as he brought his lips over Raze's dick.

As it turned out, Raze's unexpected orgasm provided him with enough self-control to keep him from burying his prick in Uriel's throat. Acknowledging the fact that this was Uriel's first time, he held still, allowing his lover to explore at his leisure. He felt a bit guilty for pushing Uriel into something he wasn't ready for, but whatever doubts he entertained faded when Uriel's tongue flicked over the head of his cock, gathering the precum leaking from the tip. He moaned, like the flavor of Raze's dick was the best thing he'd ever tasted. The vibrations of the sound combined with the tiny shocks of electricity that Uriel sent out, creating a cocktail of sensation that threatened to shatter what little composure Raze had managed to keep.

Taking a deep breath, Raze fed his cock into Uriel's mouth. Uriel's eyes widened, but he welcomed Raze in as eagerly as he responded to each of Raze's touches. At the corner of his mind, Raze recalled his experience with the VR Uriel. His imagined lover might have been awfully good at deep-throating, but he had nothing on this real-life Uriel. The pure wonder and bliss on his face held more seduction than coy smiles ever could.

Threading his fingers through Uriel's soft locks, Raze started to fuck Uriel's mouth, first slowly, then faster and faster. He tried to give Uriel some room to breathe, but at the end of the day, he was only a man, and one assaulted by sensation. The sound of his balls slapping against Uriel's chin, mixed with Uriel's muffled cries and his own groans, created a carnal symphony that added to Raze's lust. The sight of Uriel's lips stretched around his dick was torn from his most pornographic dreams. How could Raze even hope to resist it?

Impossibly, the volcanic heat of Uriel's mouth soon made yet another orgasm burn in Raze's balls. As much as he wanted to shoot his seed in Uriel's wet cavern, Raze knew better than to get overly optimistic. He'd already come once, and when he did so again, he wanted it to be inside Uriel. With a great deal of regret, he pulled out, all the while reminding his throbbing prick that he had a better destination in mind for it.

Uriel didn't seem to care about Raze's intentions. He released a keening sound, greedily trying to reach for his prize. When he looked at Raze, hot hunger burned in his now deep green eyes. His full lips were puffy from his enthusiastic sucking, and Raze had never seen him more beautiful.

Raze grabbed Uriel's hands, lest his lover accidentally seduce him into throwing his plan out the window. He pushed

Uriel down and climbed on top of him again, rubbing his cock against Uriel's.

As their dicks slid against one another, Raze bit down on Uriel's earlobe, making the younger man moan. Maddened by the sound, by Uriel's scent and touch, Raze whispered, "Uriel, I want to fuck you. I want to be inside you. Will you let me?"

Uriel didn't hesitate in the slightest. A small desperate sob escaped him, and he said, "Yes…. Oh, please, Raze. Please, please…. Take me."

With shaky hands, Raze reached for his nightstand—or rather, for the lubricant dispenser waiting there. It had been a long time since he'd used it outside his less-than-satisfying masturbating sessions, but he couldn't attribute his nervousness to his unexciting recent personal history. His lover's words made him more aware of how much this meant for Uriel. Raze couldn't fuck it up. He had to make this experience the best one in Uriel's life, to show him how meaningful the union between two bodies and two souls could be—and that he'd always be pure, no matter what happened.

After squirting a generous amount of the liquid in his palm, Raze spread Uriel's legs and rubbed the lubricant over Uriel's opening. Uriel tensed slightly when Raze dared to test the tiny hole with one finger, so Raze slowed down. He brushed his lips over Uriel's, then started to pepper Uriel's perfect face with kisses. Since Raze had been forced to free Uriel's hands, his lover responded by wrapping his arms around Raze and trying to pull him closer. Wherever his fingers touched, shocks of pleasure burst through Raze, awakening every atom of his being.

He couldn't bear it—well, almost. He had to bear it, because he desperately ached to bury his cock inside Uriel's welcoming channel. But first, he needed to help Uriel relax, and he had the perfect way to do it.

Sneaking out of Uriel's hold, Raze began to kiss down the younger man's chest. Uriel's nipples drew him away from his more immediate target. He sucked one of the tiny buds into his mouth, all the while continuing to rub his fingers over Uriel's anus. The angle wasn't perfect, but Uriel seemed quite limber as he instinctively lifted his legs, providing Raze with better access. Raze took that as encouragement, and he continued his suction on the tender bit of flesh in his mouth.

As Uriel's cries escalated, Raze's urgency exponentially increased. He found himself forced to free Uriel's nipple, largely because a different part of Uriel demanded his attention.

Tracing the taut lines of Uriel's abdomen, he finally reached Uriel's dick. Unlike Uriel, he didn't tease. He took Uriel's dick all the way into his throat, then moved back up, working his tongue just so over the thickest vein of the shaft. He'd always loved blowjobs, both giving and receiving them. It was, at the most visceral level, an exchange of raw, carnal pleasure that Raze could never resist. He wanted to show it to Uriel too.

And okay, he might not be completely selfless in this—since he desperately wanted a taste of Uriel—but he was fairly certain his lover wouldn't mind.

As he bobbed his head up and down, Raze used his free hand to roll Uriel's testicles in his palm. He took Uriel's cock deep, burying his nose in his lover's bush and inhaling the deep, fresh scent of masculinity and innocence that defined Uriel. For about ten seconds, Uriel actually tried to stop him, perhaps remembering his earlier episode during the healing process. Raze ceased his ministrations on Uriel's testicles to pet his lover's hip in a wordless attempt to comfort him. The shower had cleaned any trace of what had happened, and Uriel had nothing to worry about.

Perhaps Uriel got the message, because he stopped any semblance of protest. He started to thrust into Raze's mouth, his erratic motions making it more than clear that he was close to climax. His body seemed to lose its ability to be tense, opening right up for Raze and drawing in his fingers with greed. In fact, at one point, he began to push into them, moaning and writhing as he tried to get more of both the suction and the penetration.

Taking advantage of Uriel's obvious desire, Raze added another finger, then another. He scissored them inside Uriel, stretching his lover and preparing him for what would follow. In the process, he found Uriel's prostate, and when he mercilessly started to rub the spongy gland, Uriel almost rocketed off the bed.

"Please!" he begged.

Raze couldn't withstand the torment any longer. As much as he'd wanted to taste Uriel's spunk, that would have to wait for another day. Deeming Uriel as ready as he was going to get, he pulled his fingers out of his lover's body and released Uriel's dick from his mouth. In quick, jerky motions, he slicked up his cock. He wanted nothing more than to thrust into the haven of Uriel's channel, but at the last moment, he changed his mind.

Rolling them over, he brought Uriel above him and met his lover's eyes, nestling his erection right against Uriel's hole. God, he was beautiful, his long golden hair in disarray, his dick bobbing in front of him, slick with precum and saliva.

By some miracle, Raze managed to find his voice. "All right," he said, distantly noting that he sounded like he'd swallowed a bunch of microchips. "You can take it as slow as you like. Don't rush. We have all the time in the world here."

Uriel didn't seem inclined to listen to Raze's advice. In fact, if Raze hadn't been holding onto his hips, he'd have likely impaled himself on Raze's cock. Electricity crackled between them, the blue sparks now visible in the air. Clinging to the final threads of his restraint, Raze slowly guided Uriel down. And as his dick pierced the guardian ring of Uriel's body, Raze knew beyond any shadow of a doubt that he could never let this man go.

URIEL KNEW little of how a sexual relationship between two men worked. The bits and pieces he'd read in his romance story provided him with the only information he had. It had fascinated him so much

119

that he'd even tried to mimic it—but nothing he could have ever done had prepared him for what it felt like to have Raze inside him.

He'd been the one to reach out to Raze and ask for this, but now he was so overwhelmed that he didn't know which way was up. He did have one clear certainty. The moment Raze's cock entered him, he understood for the first time what it was like to truly feel like a person.

Oh, it hurt. In fact, it hurt like hell. Raze might have used plenty of lubricant, but his girth was far more generous than the fingers he'd had up Uriel's ass. Even so, Uriel didn't care. The burn cleared his mind, making everything so much better, more real.

Uriel tried to shove himself onto Raze's prick, but Raze had other ideas. His jaw clenched, Raze tightened his hold on Uriel's hips, keeping him from taking what he wanted. Uriel would have protested, told Raze that he could handle it, but when he opened his mouth to do just that, only a pathetic little whimper escaped him.

In the end, he could do nothing but surrender to Raze's will. He forced himself to relax, focusing on the deep black of Raze's eyes. It was those dark pools that anchored him, keeping him from going adrift in a world that was melting and cracking around him.

Inch by excruciating inch, Raze pushed inside him, and with every individual second, Uriel lost himself more and more, shuddering and choking. He felt so full, impossibly so, and he thought that surely he'd reached his limit. A heartbeat later, Raze proved him wrong, piercing him deeper, always deeper.

At one point, Uriel didn't know what to feel or what to think. Could he even think anymore? It was too hard. He couldn't identify anything but the heat of Raze's erection branding him from the inside out. When Raze stopped, having fully impaled him, Uriel took a few deep gulps of air. It was too good, too perfect. Surely no human being could survive a pleasure so intense. He needed a moment, a single moment to make sure this was truly happening.

Raze stilled inside him, clutching Uriel's hips in an ironlike vise. For the longest time, he remained that way, completely motionless. If he hadn't known better, Uriel would have thought the other man didn't feel affected at all by their position. But the look in Raze's eyes betrayed him, telling Uriel exactly how much Raze wanted him.

It was that look and the pure, naked need within it that made Uriel snap out of his trance. Supporting himself on Raze's chest, he nodded, hoping his lover would understand his wordless plea.

Raze did. Loosening his hold on Uriel's hips, he pulled out of Uriel's channel and thrust back up. Uriel had thought it couldn't get any better, but the motion made his lover's dick strike his prostate.

Sheer bliss exploded over Uriel, and whatever mistaken idea of limits had been holding him back shattered, melting away into pure want. Every atom in his body came alive with energy. Uriel felt it now, the power that had allowed him to heal Lucius Hartman. It reached out to Raze like a live thing, an extension of Uriel's yearning to be one with his lover. Uriel embraced it, embraced his desire for this man, and threw all caution to the wind. Following his instincts, he lifted his hips, then shoved himself back down onto Raze's cock.

Raze's grip on him tightened again, to the point of pain, but unlike before, he didn't try to temper Uriel's enthusiasm. The time for patience and waiting had long gone. Instead, he thrust up inside him so hard Uriel's teeth rattled.

Uriel loved it, loved every beautifully painful moment of it. He met Raze's every motion, and they fell into a fluid yet desperate rhythm. Their bodies came together in the most intimate dance of all time, but so did their souls. Uriel felt it, felt Raze so deep inside, and not only at a physical level but all the way into his heart. Then again, Raze had already snuck into Uriel's soul. Uriel had just been too afraid to accept it.

He accepted it now, because there was no way he could deny it. At one point, he'd fallen in love with the leader of the cyborg resistance—no, with Raze. It didn't matter that they belonged to different worlds, that their roles in society had made them out to be enemies. Right now, they were just two men, living and loving, making their own rules from the emotions they shared.

Uriel clung to that thought for a while longer, until it too dissipated in the heat building up between them. With each of Raze's thrusts inside him, his coherence and reason melted into pure instinct, until his mind could only focus on a single idea. *Yes, please. More, Raze. Raze. Raze. Raze.*

The sensations escalated to a point where he knew he would not be able to last for much longer. He hovered over something momentous, on the lip of an abyss he couldn't wait to plunge into. He just needed one more thing, one last thing to propel him over the edge.

As if guessing his thoughts, Raze reached for Uriel's dick. Two strokes of Raze's hand, and it was all over. Pleasure swallowed Uriel whole, wild, uncontrollable, raw, a whirlpool of sensation and emotion that threatened to stop his heart. He arched his back and came, shooting jets of white spunk all over his lover's chest.

The ecstasy felt so intense it would have been scary, but Raze was right there with him. He thrust inside Uriel one more time, and then, with a grunt, found his own peak, filling Uriel with his seed. They shook together through the waves of their shared orgasm, lost in a world where only the two of them existed, one created out of pure passion and desire. Hundreds of bolts of electricity rushed over him in a thunderstorm of lust and fulfillment that melded two souls and bodies together into one cohesive whole.

It seemed to go on and on, and yet it ended far too soon. As the aftershocks of the explosive pleasure began to settle, Uriel slumped down on top of Raze, uncaring that he lay in his own spunk. A comfortable exhaustion fell over him, so much so that he didn't even wince when Raze slid out of him.

Raze chuckled and kissed his forehead. "That was amazing, baby."

Uriel couldn't have agreed more. In fact, he would have loved to attempt a repeat performance, had his body not reminded him that he had his limits after all.

Still, when Raze left the bed, Uriel found the strength to protest. "Don't worry," Raze soothed him. "I'm just going to the bathroom."

Indeed, Raze returned moments later with a cloth likely moistened in the steam shower. He wiped Uriel down with the same care he'd used earlier. His gentleness contrasted sharply with the near-violence he'd fucked Uriel with, but that only made it more meaningful, more powerful. It also solidified Uriel's realization that he'd fallen head over heels in love with Raze.

He wanted to say it, but the words refused to come out. And when Raze threw the cloth away and returned to the bed, Uriel simply couldn't bring himself to shatter the moment with heartfelt declarations that might not be well received. He cuddled by his lover's side, enjoying Raze's heat and feeling safer than he had in his entire life. Raze petted his hair, and Uriel closed his eyes, ready to drift into slumber.

He was about to fall asleep when a loud knock sounded at the door. "Open the damn door, Raze," Logan said from outside. "You really need to see something."

Raze frowned, looking like he was going to protest the interruption. However, something in Logan's voice told Uriel that this couldn't be delayed. "Let him in," he told his lover. "This must be important."

Raze complied, probably realizing Logan's urgency as well. He slid out of the bed and unlocked the door. Uriel barely had time to cover his nakedness with the blanket before Logan burst inside.

His sudden attack of modesty turned out to be useless, because Logan didn't seem to even notice his nudity. The moment he stepped inside, he turned on the monitor mounted on the wall. "We sent in the message, like we discussed," he explained, "and then this happened."

Uriel stared at the image, feeling like the beautiful dream of Raze's affection for him was already shattering around him. Any thought of sleep had vanished. Right there, on the screen, was a live feed from the Temple of Genesis agora. On the same platform where a few days ago Uriel had blessed thousands of believers, his mother now stood—and by her side was Uriel.

Chapter Eight

THROUGHOUT THE years he'd spent as the leader of the resistance, Raze had run into a lot of challenges. He'd taken everything in stride and had more or less managed to handle the surprises well.

But nothing had prepared him for seeing Uriel on the monitor of the vid-screen while his lover still lay on the bed that had been the witness of their spent passions. "This can't be a live feed," he said, drawing the first logical conclusion. "It must be a recording of a past ceremonial day."

Logan shook his head. "I traced the signal. It's coming from the agora, crystal clear. I truly would have thought it to be a trick of sorts, but just listen to what they're saying."

Raze did, and he instantly realized what his friend meant. Councilwoman Abigail—Uriel's mother and supposed Guardian—was in the middle of quite a speech.

"The attack tonight proves what we've known all along, that the machine-people are incredibly dangerous. We've been fighting the so-called resistance for years, but now they've shown their true face in trying to harm our beloved Guiding Light. Mercifully, their plan failed, and he is still here with us, but had our forces not intervened, tragedy could have struck." She paused for effect and gestured for the second Uriel to approach. The young man did and then stood next to her like an automaton. "Something has to be done," Abigail continued. "We have been merciful to these inferior machine-people, but we can no longer afford mercy."

The hundreds of purists gathered in the agora cheered and roared. "Death to the machine-people! Death! Death!"

It didn't take a genius to connect all the dots. "Fuck. No wonder security practically allowed us in. We were supposed to take him out."

"We thought they wouldn't risk any harm coming to their precious Guiding Light," Logan said, "but we missed one very distinct possibility. They cloned him."

Raze threw a glance toward the bed, where his lover still lay curled, quiet as the grave. He couldn't imagine what Uriel must be going through right now. He had shouldered such responsibilities, thinking he alone could fulfill the demands of the position of the Guiding Light. He'd suffered through pain and torture, all because he had believed his role and purpose to be true. And now it turned out that he was merely another expendable toy, a tool in the hands of the purists. To top it off, cloning had long ago been banned, and it seemed impossible that the purists, with all their nontech ways, would resurrect the method.

Even realizing how much this situation could harm the resistance, Raze couldn't help but be first and foremost concerned for his lover. Turning away from the monitor, he rushed back to Uriel's side. "Uriel? Are you all right?"

For a few moments, Uriel said nothing. He didn't even look at Raze. His fists clenched in the blanket as he stared at the screen. Something inside Raze cracked at seeing him like that, especially after they'd shared such a beautiful experience.

"Uriel?" he asked again.

At last his lover snapped out of his trance. "I'm fine. I... I want to know. There's more, right?"

The question was addressed to Logan, and when Raze looked over his shoulder, he saw his friend scowling fiercely.

"Perhaps you should say it, not me. I'm not even—"

"Just say it," Uriel said, interrupting Logan's answer. "Please."

Logan stared at Uriel in disbelief, like he couldn't believe what he was hearing. Turning toward Raze, he released a heavy sigh. "I think I'd better show you. Come to the workshop. I'll wait for you there."

With those enigmatic words, Logan stalked out of the room. As soon as his friend was gone, Raze took Uriel's now-cold hands in his own and squeezed them tightly. "What made you guess Logan wasn't telling you something?"

Uriel's Adam's apple bobbed as he swallowed nervously. "I don't really know. Your friend.... He's the one who guessed something wasn't right. I get the feeling he might have some answers for us."

For whatever reason, Raze didn't look forward to hearing those answers. Nonetheless, this was important for his lover, so Raze went along with it. He helped Uriel dress in the garments he'd found earlier. He'd managed to procure some footwear that wouldn't be so hard on Uriel's delicate feet, and his efforts didn't go unnoticed. In fact, they actually drew a small smile out of his lover. It encouraged Raze, and he tried to tell himself that everything would be all right, that together they could turn this unexpected ploy of the purists against them. In the end, cloning was a crime, and maybe if they got the rest of the Edenians to see the truth, it would be an advantage for Raze's people.

He didn't know if he believed that, so he refrained from offering Uriel encouraging words that would mean nothing. He took Uriel's hand in his own and guided him out of the room. As the door slid closed behind them, Raze had the strangest feeling that they'd left their sanctuary of love behind to venture into the unknown.

By rights, he shouldn't have felt that way, because they were still in the resistance headquarters and the purists had yet to attack them. However, his men had obviously learned about this new development and were no longer so enthusiastic about Uriel's stay.

No sooner had Raze descended to the first floor of their hideout than Hugh intercepted him, glaring angrily. "You played right into their hands, didn't you, boy?" he exploded at Raze. "In fact, you probably took their defective Guiding Light off their hands, just in time to allow them to replace him with a new, less carnally inclined one."

Raze barely managed to contain his anger at the unfair comment. He would have punched the older cyborg had Uriel not stopped him.

"If wanting Raze is my sin, then I will own up to it," Uriel said. "I'm not ashamed of what the two of us have. But arguing about it now is not going to help us. Whatever Councilwoman Abigail thinks, I still have some power, and we can't let them win."

Raze hadn't thought he could feel more proud of Uriel than he already did, but yet again, Uriel was proving him wrong and surprising him with his strength. Hugh seemed just as taken aback, but the shock didn't keep him distracted for long. He would have probably delivered a scathing retort, but Raze's father intervened before the conversation could go any further.

He supported himself on Julian's shoulder, but nonetheless he was standing and walking, which, given his condition just a few hours back, seemed to be a miracle. "Back off, Hugh," he said. "I don't know much about this situation, but I do know the boy saved my life, and he's on our side."

Hugh stared at Raze's father in disbelief. His mouth worked open and closed as he did an interesting imitation of a fish. If he'd heard about Raze's father's recovery, he must have believed it to be more moderate.

"Lucius… I can't believe this. Did he really… I didn't think it was possible."

"It probably wasn't," Raze answered, "not without Uriel's help. And now, if you're done spouting your venom, we're needed elsewhere."

They pushed past Hugh and headed toward the medical wing, where Logan had earlier scanned Uriel for any hidden tracking devices. When they reached their destination, they found the other cyborg poring over some papers. "Secure the room," Logan said without looking at them. "I don't want anyone to listen in."

Raze wordlessly complied, punching some commands in the panel next to the door. Once Raze finished his task, Logan faced them, his gaze immediately zeroing in on Uriel. "Anything you'd like to share with us before I speak?"

Judging by the tightness in his voice, he was more convinced than ever of Uriel's supposed malice. Uriel squeezed Raze's hand tighter and straightened his back. "No, but I will hear you out."

"Fair enough, although personally, I think that, at the very least, Raze deserves to know the truth from your mouth." He paused, as if giving Uriel the chance to defend himself. When Uriel said nothing, Logan angrily threw the papers in Uriel's face. "What do you have to say for yourself?"

Raze stepped in, keeping the barrage of documents from hitting his lover. "What's going on, Logan?" he asked. "You know Uriel couldn't have known about the clone."

"It's not about the fucking clone," Logan practically growled. "Just look and you'll understand what I mean."

Raze was rapidly losing his patience with his friend's erratic behavior. But Logan had never failed him, so Raze had to give the other cyborg the benefit of the doubt. He picked up the pages Logan had thrown and scanned them, trying to make sense of the data on the printouts.

The images showed a shot of a DNA sequence, although it appeared to have some strange errors. Most significantly, instead of two strands of DNA, there were three. Judging by Logan's behavior, the DNA belonged to Uriel.

"This can't be right," Raze said. "There must be some mistake."

"No mistake," Logan replied, suddenly sounding very tired. "I stole one of your lover's locks of hair and analyzed it more closely. Before the damn machine short-circuited, I managed to get those results and print them out. That's an image of your Uriel's DNA. Earlier, I thought I could be wrong, but the more I look at the damn thing, the more convinced I am that I'm right."

"Assuming this is true, what conclusions have you drawn from these results?" Uriel asked, his voice now sounding very distant and aloof.

"Do you truly not know?" Logan asked. "Or can't you guess? Surely you must suspect by now, even if you didn't before—which I highly doubt."

"You mean to say that I'm genetically engineered, and this third strand of DNA is the source of my power," Uriel replied.

"There's more to it than that," Logan replied. "If I'm right, and I have every reason to believe that I am, you're not only a genetic experiment. You are a weapon, one that was created to destroy the cyborgs. You, Uriel, are the virus that destroyed us all."

WHAT DOES a person do when he finds out he was responsible for the death and pain of millions of people? Cry? Scream? Throw up? Uriel wanted to do all that. He wanted to deny Logan's conclusion and explain it wasn't possible. And yet, in his heart, he couldn't dismiss Logan's words.

Raze apparently had every intention of doing just that. "You're crazy. How could Uriel be the virus? He's a human being."

"Stop denying it, Raze," Logan shot back. "You know we always wondered how it was possible for a virus to propel itself through all the implants, when there shouldn't have been a network between them. That's what your lover did. He was created for the very specific purpose of connecting the implants, and once he had the ID chip implanted, the new link reacted to the unnatural energy, short-circuiting everything. And of course, after that, it was so easy for the purists to take over and create a new world order. After all, no leader in his right mind would dare to go against the Guiding Light."

It was true, and it made so much sense it hurt. Uriel might live in Eden, in a country built around the idea of him, but other peoples came to see him too. They had ceremonial days, just for them, set aside from the ones dedicated to the citizens of Eden. More than once, world leaders had come to see Uriel in the hope of being soothed of their ailments. Eden was easily the greatest power in the world—all because they had Uriel. And Uriel definitely considered his so-called mother capable of scheming this elaborate ploy, if only because she'd never seen him as a person.

Uriel struggled to breathe and not fall into a panic attack. Guilt threatened to smother him, but he buried it deep inside, focusing on what he could do now to fix the situation.

Some things could never be mended, but dwelling on that wouldn't help them. Uriel closed his eyes and slowly allowed himself to drift in that mental state that allowed him endure the ceremonial days. He would carry the burden of the past, but that didn't free him from the weight of the present, and of the future.

When he opened his eyes, he'd found the strength he needed to deal with the knowledge of the blood on his hands. "There's no reason to discuss this now," he said calmly. "It might be true or it might not. It doesn't matter."

Logan stared at him in shock. "It doesn't matter?" he repeated. "What kind of monster are you? Do you have any idea how many people died worldwide because—"

"Yes, I know," Uriel cut him off. "But do you want to die too? That's going to happen if we don't act now, if we don't fight the Council. Whatever they're planning, it's bigger than wiping out the resistance. I know it."

At last Raze found his voice. "Uriel is right. This stays between us. We have other priorities."

"I hate to say it, but you're probably correct." Logan rubbed his eyes tiredly. "I can't even imagine the ramifications should this information come to light. In any case, I don't suppose you have any ideas on how to fight back?"

"Actually," Uriel said, "I do. But you're going to have to trust me."

Chapter Nine

A few hours later

THE AGORA of the Temple of Genesis was crawling with guards armed to the teeth. The purist citizens had long ago been dispersed and told to stay indoors as the armed forces roamed the streets of the ghettoes and started arrests.

Raze lay crouched in the shadow of a building, knowing all too well that the fate of the cyborgs in Eden depended on the success of their mission. A niggling part of him reminded him that this might have never happened if he hadn't decided to kidnap Uriel. Hugh had said as much, as had the accusing glances other cyborgs threw his way. Some of the aggression had dwindled now, but that hadn't come without a price.

Raze threw a glance toward Uriel, and the fist clenching his heart tightened even further. In the darkness, Uriel looked impossibly pale, like a ghost haunting the night. He still managed to offer Raze a small smile, but that only made Raze hurt more.

He didn't know how, but Uriel had managed to reboot the implants of every single cyborg in the resistance. Unlike in Raze's case, each individual reboot had been taxing on Uriel. While not as difficult as what Uriel had done for Raze's father, when added up,

133

healing two hundred cyborgs had drained Uriel. Raze suspected it was only sheer willpower—and maybe a hefty dose of guilt—that kept Uriel standing.

"You doing okay?" he asked his lover.

"Fine," Uriel mouthed at him. "Don't worry about me. I'm stronger than I look."

That might have been the case, but Raze would have still liked to leave him behind somewhere safe. Sadly, he didn't know what was safe anymore. Not to mention that they needed Uriel for the success of their plan.

Forcing himself to focus on the mission, Raze turned toward the agora once more. He scanned the darkness, searching for patterns and weak spots in the movements of the patrols. As Raze's mental computer processed the data he fed into it through his advanced senses, Logan made his way to his side, followed by the group he was in charge of.

"We found an entry point on the other side of the agora," he whispered. "It's being watched, but not as avidly as the other areas."

"No," Uriel said adamantly. "I know the entrance of which you speak, and it's not safe."

"How can you be so sure?" Logan inquired. Somehow, even if both of them were whispering, Raze could hear the tension in their voices.

"That's the entrance my mother expects me to use. When I lived here as a child, I once sneaked out of the temple through it— and it's still the one we regularly go through when I'm brought to Genesis. They'll be waiting for us there."

"They've done that before," Raze pointed out, "when we first snuck into the compound. We can't play into their hands again."

Logan nodded, perhaps realizing that now was not the time to take out his frustrations on Uriel. "Do you have an alternative route, then?" he asked.

Raze pointed to the area he'd been scanning and grinned. "Through the front door."

"We'll stick to what we discussed," Uriel offered. "I will create a distraction for you. It's the best way, and we can take them head on."

Logan blanched but didn't protest. He crawled by Raze's side and looked into the distance at the clusters of purist guards. "Sounds crazy. Crazy enough to work."

It meant a lot to Raze that, for all his obvious displeasure with the situation, Logan still had his back. He wished things were different and Logan understood how Raze felt about Uriel, but that would never happen—especially if he was right with regard to the root source of the virus.

For his part, Raze still didn't blame Uriel for the destruction it had caused. For crying out loud, Uriel had only been a baby. He'd been used, and if anyone held the responsibility for what had happened, it was the people they were trying to stop. Uriel was a victim, just like the countless cyborgs who'd died twenty years earlier.

Falling back into the mind-set he used whenever he was on a mission, Raze internalized the data his mental computer processed. His plan was dangerous indeed, but Uriel had given them back the use of their implants, which made them faster and stronger than the purists. They'd probably need it, because the sensors and security systems of the Temple could kill them before they even stepped inside.

Of course, the hardest task lay on Uriel's shoulders. Swallowing around the knot in his throat, Raze threw a glance toward his lover. "Ready?"

"Always," Uriel replied. "Let's do this."

Without looking at anyone, Uriel slid out of his clothes, since they'd decided that the garments shattered the illusion they'd try to create. Now naked, he sneaked away from the group of gathered cyborgs.

Raze watched him go, a silent shadow, all alone in front of the people he'd once considered his allies. He couldn't help but wince when he noticed Uriel start to limp as his bare feet came into contact with the ground. Unfortunately the purists had adopted an old-fashioned style in terms of pathways, and the irregular pavement in the agora proved to be yet another painful obstacle for Uriel.

What had possessed Raze to agree with this again? He couldn't bear it. He couldn't stand around and watch how the man he loved tortured himself to atone for a crime he hadn't committed.

He got up, ready to rush after Uriel and stop this madness. At the last moment, Logan grabbed his arm and held him back, shaking his head. "This is our only chance," he reminded Raze. "Don't ruin it."

Raze really wanted to punch his friend. He wanted to break something, scream at the injustice, and tear the purists apart with his bare hands. He wanted to wrap his arms around Uriel and never let him go, to protect him, just like he had promised. But the only way to do that now was to wait. And so Raze settled down at the edge of the agora, holding his breath and watching as his lover made his way toward the temple.

In mere seconds, the guards noticed his approach. "Halt!" someone shouted. "Who goes there?"

"Help me," Uriel called out. "Help me, Simon. Please."

Raze assumed Simon was the guard who'd called out into the darkness. It was a good thing they'd run into someone Uriel knew personally. It would give them an advantage, something they could exploit.

"Your Holiness?" the same voice asked in shock. "What.... What happened to you?"

Dozens of guards approached Uriel, some more cautiously, others running toward him, stumbling over their feet in their need to assist the Guiding Light in distress. It seemed obvious that most of the underlings hadn't been told of a possible second Guiding Light, something which Raze had been counting on.

He signaled for Logan to take his team around the other side of the agora while he and his men began their approach. By now Uriel had slumped down on the ground, cradling his bleeding feet. Alarmed shouts sounded all around the area, and it was only a matter of time until the clone came out of the temple or someone notified the Council of Uriel's arrival.

It was also a good thing that the purist guards couldn't touch Uriel, which meant they couldn't grab him or even pick him up. Still, they now formed a barrier between Raze and Uriel—and that was something Raze could not allow.

Already aching for his lover, Raze took advantage of the distraction Uriel had provided and signaled for the attack to begin. His men and Logan's hit at the same time, from opposite directions. At first the purist soldiers didn't realize they were being taken out, but then the sensors began to scream wildly. The guards drew deadly phasers as they prepared to fight back. For all the panic Uriel's appearance had triggered, the soldiers now responded to the attack with professionalism and precision as they attempted to keep Raze's forces at bay.

Raze wasn't too worried about the soldiers. His armor managed to withstand the attack, and his men had so far avoided any deadly blows. Being a large, wide-open space, the agora didn't provide the soldiers with many hiding spots. But that turned out to be a serious problem when the ground in front of the temple opened up, revealing a huge automated plasma cannon.

Now in the middle of the agora, Raze and his men had no place to hide from the blast. "Get down!" Raze shouted.

As he dropped to the ground, a wave of shock bolts swept over the area. It didn't spare anyone—the purist soldiers who were struck dropped down, in all likelihood dead. Most of the cyborgs managed to avoid being hit, but much to his horror, Raze noted one of the shock bolts heading straight for Logan.

Its angle was such that Logan couldn't dodge it or evade it the way Raze had. Raze wanted to shout a warning, to do anything that would help his friend, but he didn't get a chance.

Everything happened so fast and yet as if in slow motion. At the very last moment, just as Raze thought Logan would be killed,

Uriel appeared out of nowhere. He threw himself in front of Logan, receiving the full brunt of the blast.

A wave of power shook the agora, and a shock of energy recoiled back from Uriel into the plasma cannon. The weapon exploded, sending bits of metal flying all over the place. Raze would have rejoiced, but not even Uriel could resist the full power of a plasma cannon blast. He collapsed on the ground like a puppet with his strings cut.

Silence fell over the agora. No one moved and no one spoke. Whatever the guards thought about the attack, they were clearly shaken at seeing their Guiding Light fall, since they made no attempt to reach for their weapons again. Raze didn't care. He couldn't care anymore. Breathless with fear, he got up and ran to his fallen lover's side.

The purist guards didn't try to stop him. He knelt at Uriel's side and turned him over, hoping against all hope that somehow, by some sort of miracle, Uriel could have survived. "Uriel?" he asked. "Baby, can you hear me?"

No reply came. Uriel didn't move, nor did he give any sign of having heard Raze. In fact, he wasn't breathing, and Raze's enhanced hearing couldn't detect a heartbeat.

No. Raze refused to accept it. Uriel couldn't be dead. It simply wasn't possible. They still had so much to share, to love, to do. This couldn't be happening. Raze had only just found him. He'd only just admitted to himself that he'd fallen in love with the man he'd once considered his worst enemy.

Logan dropped by his side, breathing hard. He stared at Uriel's fallen figure, as if he couldn't understand why Uriel would have sacrificed himself for him. Raze didn't even look at him. With an angry snarl, he started to perform fast compressions on Uriel's chest. When he reached thirty, he pressed his mouth to Uriel's and forced air into Uriel's lungs, then repeated the process. "Come on, baby. Come on. Work with me. Come back. I know you can do it."

He was so distracted by his goal that he didn't even realize the guards had finally snapped out of their trance. Logan cursed as he shot a bolt of energy over Raze's shoulder. "Raze, come on. Take him and let's head inside. We can't stay here any longer. We have to finish the mission."

At some level, Raze understood the words, but he didn't really process them. He knew he had to keep going, that somehow he could bring his lover back. Everything else was irrelevant.

The part of Raze's brain that remained a machine registered that Uriel was dead. His mental computer swirled around that concept, repeating the word over and over. *Error: Dead. Error: Dead. Error: Dead.* Nothing else could compute, because his rational side had remained fixed on that.

But Raze's human heart wouldn't allow him to let go. "Come on, baby," he repeated. "Don't do this. Don't leave me."

The taste of despair and grief filled his mouth, quickly shrouded by a denial that refused to allow him to acknowledge his loss. He picked Uriel up in his arms, fully intending to rush back to the resistance headquarters. They had equipment there that could keep Uriel alive, maybe even help him recover.

Unfortunately, Raze couldn't retreat now, since more and more purist guards were surrounding them. They might have actually died there, but then the unlikeliest thing happened.

Suddenly Uriel's eyes shot open, and a blast of energy emanated from him toward the purist soldiers. They were pushed back by the shock wave, but by some sort of miracle, the cyborgs still fighting weren't affected. In fact, the ones who'd been struck by the phasers of the guards got up, shaking themselves and already steady on their feet.

Uriel didn't appear to realize that he'd spent the past few minutes basically dead. "Quickly," he said. "We have to go inside. We don't have much time."

Raze could have kissed him. In fact, he did exactly that, uncaring that they were, indeed, still at risk. He just knew that

Uriel's heart had begun to beat steadily again and that he was alive and miraculously unharmed.

To reassure himself of this, Raze thrust his tongue into Uriel's mouth, reveling in the feel of him, so warm, so alive, so his. In spite of his previous words, Uriel melted against him, moaning as he met Raze's tongue with his own.

They would have probably lost themselves in their shared desire—in spite of the less than ideal situation—but Logan tapped his shoulder. Raze broke the kiss and faced his friend, expecting a reprimand. It did come, but not in the way he'd become accustomed to. "I know you deserve to have a little moment to yourselves," he said, "but we really have to go. Any moment now, reinforcements will arrive. We have to take advantage of the chance Uriel gave us."

Raze saw what Logan meant when he looked past the fallen purist guards at the open gateway. He didn't wait for another invitation. Still carrying Uriel, he rushed toward the entrance with Logan and his men following behind him.

They didn't get very far before they ran into the exact people they'd been looking for. Councilwoman Abigail, together with a few other Council members, cut them off. To a certain extent, Raze was surprised at the daring—he'd expected to have to hunt them down through the entire temple. Of course, the Council members' decision probably had something to do with the fact that a significant number of guards surrounded them, forming a barrier between Raze's group and the Council members.

"Well, well…." Abigail said with a smirk. "This is quite an interesting surprise. I suppose I should welcome you home… son."

Uriel squeezed Raze's arm, and Raze set his lover down. An outburst of protectiveness made him take off his jacket and wrap it around Uriel's shoulders.

"Stop this, Mother. You know as well as I do that the cyborgs aren't the ones to blame for the disaster of our world."

140

"Is that right?" a man Raze recognized as Ezekiel Zion asked. "I believe that we will be far safer once blasphemer machine-people are gone. Not only do you attempt to hurt our Guiding Light, but you create a sickening copy of him."

As Ezekiel spoke, the second Uriel made his appearance, stepping up next to his so-called parents. "I don't know who you people are," he said softly, "but being the Guiding Light is a serious responsibility. You should be ashamed of yourselves for taking advantage of it."

"I wonder if you truly believe that," Uriel replied softly, wrapping himself tighter in Raze's jacket. "I did for a long time, and when I stopped believing, I was discarded. Your memories are mine, young Guiding Light. I know all your pain, all your burdens, and I know you can't carry them for purist citizens alone. Cyborgs have the right to live and love too."

"Your beloved cyborgs have been pulling us back for years now," Ezekiel spat. "The tech they still cling to pollutes the world we are trying to build. They need to disappear, but they stubbornly refuse to do so."

"You forget one very simple thing, Ezekiel Zion," Raze answered. "We're the ones who work to support your lavish lifestyles."

Ezekiel snorted. "You are only worthy of being slaves, nothing more."

"You're wrong," Uriel piped up steadily. "Cyborgs are people too, and you can no longer treat them like this."

"And I'm guessing your... epiphany has a lot to do with the man behind you." Abigail sneered. "You disgust me. Guards, destroy them."

"Wait!" the second Uriel tried to say. "Please—"

It was too late. The purist soldiers were already in motion. They reached for their blasters, setting them at full voltage. At the same time, hundreds of miniature plasma cannons appeared from the walls. Raze had expected it, as Uriel had warned him beforehand that the security systems of the Temple of Genesis were not to be trifled with.

What he did not expect was his lover lifting a hand and finishing the second Uriel's phrase. "Please stop," he said simply. "There's already been too much sorrow and death. It has to end now."

Energy crackled at Uriel's fingertips, and the entire area lit up, a blinding glow surrounding them all. To Raze, it felt warm, almost loving, but he suspected the purist guards didn't experience it the same way. With choked gasps, they crumpled to the floor, their weapons falling next to them, useless. Similarly, the plasma cannons released protesting beeps and went dead.

The only one who held his ground was the second Uriel, who must have been immune to Uriel's power. Abigail, on the other hand, collapsed, just like the guards. "H-how?" she stammered.

"You underestimated me, Mother," Uriel replied. "I'm stronger now. Raze gave me more than you can ever imagine. You can't control me anymore. I will stop you."

Much to Raze's shock, Ezekiel started to laugh. "It's too late now. In a few minutes your precious ghettoes will be no more. Whatever you think you've accomplished will be futile. The countdown for the missile launch has already started. You can't stop it."

The second Uriel's eyes widened. "No. You can't be serious."

"They are," Raze's lover answered. "That was the whole point of this entire setup, to destroy the resistance, to turn the remaining Edenian cyborgs into slaves. We need to go to the command center. It's our only chance."

Uriel's clone didn't argue with them. Apparently some things never changed, and in spite of his not being the real Uriel, he still had that same kindness that had made Raze fall in love with the original Guiding Light. "This way. Quickly. We have to prevent the launch."

Raze couldn't have agreed more. His brother and his father had stayed behind to make sure the younger members of the resistance didn't get caught by the purist forces. However, their efforts would be for naught if the Council indeed planned to bomb the entire area.

Raze and his men followed behind the two Uriels—and God, one could go crazy just thinking about that. They descended several flights of stairs and several times ran into more automated weaponry or clusters of guards. Seeing both Guiding Lights together made the soldiers back off. It wasn't so easy with the weapons, but Uriel's new power—which Raze could only assume might have something to do with the plasma blast he'd taken to his chest—handled it.

Still, it seemed to take them forever to reach the command center deep beneath the Temple of Genesis. Oddly enough, Raze's Uriel didn't know the way, but the clone did, which Raze guessed might mean there had been more movement around the command center in the period since Uriel had left.

Or so he thought, until the clone proceeded to explain, "My current quarters are down here. I've become pretty well accustomed to the area."

As he ran, Raze passed a room with a small inscription: "GenL." For someone unaccustomed to implant technology, it didn't mean anything, but Raze's brain immediately translated it into Genetics Lab.

Some sort of instinct made Raze burst into the room. He was not disappointed by what he found. Something that looked a lot like a cyber tube lay open, with hundreds of cables trailing from it onto the floor. It didn't take a genius to figure out that this must have been the place where Uriel's clone, if not Uriel himself, had been created.

Two scientists were still inside the room, manning the computers. The duo turned toward Raze, their eyes widening. "Wait! You can't be in here."

Raze pushed them aside, completely ignoring their protests. Uriel was already sitting down in front of the computers. "This will do, I think," he said. "Logan, take the others and go forward to the command center. I'll stay here and try to access it remotely."

"I'll come with you," Uriel's clone offered. "One of us is bound to be able to stop the launch."

As the rest of the group continued on their way, Raze remained by Uriel's side. Uriel took a deep breath and closed his eyes, his fingers hovering over the keyboard. He wasn't touching the smooth slate of the device, and yet the letters and numbers on it lit up, like they would have had someone been typing away.

On the screens, images and numbers flashed so quickly Raze had trouble registering them all. Even with his mental computer's processor working at full speed, he couldn't take in all the data Uriel was sifting through. The rush stopped for a few moments when the search ran into an encrypted folder that said "Project Uriel." Alarms blared as "Access Denied" flared onto the screen several times. In the end, Uriel bypassed the security protocols, revealing several images that looked very much like the printout Logan had showed them. One look at the formulas that accompanied the image made Raze sick to his stomach and told him Logan had been right in his earlier guess.

Uriel released a choked sob but didn't otherwise falter. The screens changed, once again starting their erratic, kaleidoscopic display. Uriel must have decided to mourn his part in this disaster later, once they made sure the threat to the ghettoes was neutralized.

Finally, a countdown appeared on the screen. Raze would have been grateful that the purists hadn't simply launched the missiles before they'd come to face his forces in battle, but it might not be an entirely good thing. There were specific missiles that had to pass through elaborate security protocols before being launched, ones that could be used to wipe out entire areas with surgical precision. And there were only two minutes left, two minutes until the ghettoes became a crater neighboring the otherwise unharmed Genesis. It was older tech but nonetheless very effective.

As the seconds ticked past, Raze began to panic. One hundred nineteen seconds…. One hundred eighteen…. One hundred seventeen…. Shit, what were they going to do?

Uriel turned toward Raze and said, "I have a confession to make, Raze."

One hundred sixteen.... Fifteen.... Fourteen....

"I love you."

Thirteen.... Twelve.... Eleven....

"Uriel, I love you too, but I don't think now is the right time—"

Before Raze could finish the sentence, Uriel got up from his seat and pressed his mouth to Raze's. Just like that, Raze's mental computer shut down, and everything went black.

URIEL HELD his lover close, his heart breaking as he realized this would be the last time he'd ever get to do so. Raze would never agree to it, of course, which was why Uriel had to knock him out.

Just like he'd known would happen, his brother stepped into the room. Some might have called him a clone, but Uriel knew the truth. He'd felt a kinship with the other man from the moment they'd met. "I don't know how, but I had the feeling you would need me," his brother said.

"I do," Uriel replied. "I need you to help me with something very important. Take Raze and get out of here. There's no stopping the launch now, and there's not enough time to change the trajectory. But I can detonate the missiles here. I just have to be in the temple to do so."

"But.... You'll die."

Uriel nodded, having already made his peace with the inevitable. "And you'll live. Love Raze in my stead, brother. You have my memories. You know who I am. You can do this."

"Are you asking me to be you?" his brother inquired.

Uriel stole a look at the screens, where the countdown kept going. "Yes. Please... I know it's a lot to ask, but there really is no other way."

145

His brother sighed heavily and nodded. Uriel supported Raze on the other man's shoulder. "Take care of him."

"I will," his sibling promised.

Without further ado, Uriel's brother left the room, supporting Raze's limp form on his shoulder. Uriel sat back down at the computers and connected with the systems of the Temple of Genesis. He started the evacuation alarms, guiding everyone toward the exits.

Through the security cameras, he watched the guards retrieve the fallen soldiers he'd earlier knocked out. The Council members—including Abigail and Ezekiel—ran out, bursting into the agora. Soon Uriel, Raze, and the rest of the cyborgs followed, taking cover where they could. Just in time too. They'd moved quickly and expediently, managing to evacuate in a single minute, but the seconds were ticking away.

Five.... Four.... Three.... This was it. Taking a deep breath, Uriel mentally sent another "I love you" to Raze and detonated the bomb.

WHEN RAZE cracked open his eyes, the first thing he saw was Uriel's beautiful figure looming above him. "Welcome back," Uriel said with a smile. "How are you doing?"

Raze grunted as his mental computer finished rebooting its drive. "I've been better. What the hell happened?"

"Don't you remember?" Uriel asked. "We were inside the Temple. We had to stop the Council from launching the missiles onto the ghettoes. All of us went to...."

Raze pressed his thumb to Uriel's lips, interrupting the explanation. The memories were still a little fuzzy, but that wasn't his focus right now.

He peered at Uriel's face, meeting those green eyes he knew so well. Only... they weren't Uriel's eyes. Identical though they might have been, those emerald orbs didn't hold the same emotion Raze saw in his lover.

"Where is Uriel?" he asked softly.

The fake Uriel laughed shakily, pulling back from him. "What are you talking about, Raze? It's me. Did you hit your head?"

Raze glared and grabbed the other man's wrist, squeezing it tightly. "Answer the question and don't fuck with me. I know you're not him. You may fool everyone else, but not me. Never me. I'll ask you one more time. Where. Is. Uriel?"

Uriel's clone finally dropped his façade. "I'm sorry," he replied. "He... he was in the temple. He wanted you to be happy."

Raze looked past the other man's shoulder, only to see the Temple of Genesis lying in ruins. Without wasting another moment, he shot to his feet and ran toward the destroyed building, his mental computer already assessing the damage and finding possible ways in.

His last memory of Uriel finally came back. "I love you, Raze," Uriel had said.

And because Raze loved Uriel too, he refused to let their story end this way. He would not give up. He'd never give up on Uriel, not while he still had breath in his body.

Of course he might actually have a problem with that, because thick smoke surrounded the entire area where the Temple of Genesis had once stood. The fire originating from the explosion had been extinguished, but the fumes still lingered in the air, making it nearly impossible for him to see or even breathe.

Using his eye implants, Raze scanned the area over and over, all the while throwing rocks aside as he tried to make his way through the rubble. Soon Logan appeared by his side, quietly assisting him in his quest. Other cyborgs joined in, perhaps realizing the reason for Raze's desperation.

At last, as Raze's still-human lungs began to protest, his enhanced eyes caught sight of something, or rather someone, underneath all the stone. A slender scorched arm seemed to reach out to him from between the crumbled bricks. Torn between fear and hope, Raze moved aside the stone—only to unveil Uriel's fallen, broken body.

GUIDING LIGHT Uriel Noah of the House of Zion watched the retrieval of the body in silence and confusion. Plopping down on a rock that had once formed part of a temple column, he tried to make sense of what was happening.

A few hours ago, everything had been so clear. He needed to uphold his duties as Guiding Light, even if the machine-people tried to attack him. His mother had given him instructions on the way he should act, some of which he'd actually found redundant. After all, it wasn't the first time he'd been in this situation, right?

And now here he was, with the knowledge that he hadn't been the Guiding Light after all, but only an imperfect copy of a man willing to sacrifice everything for the people he loved.

Where did that leave him? Everyone seemed to have forgotten about him entirely. Most cyborgs were rounding up the staff of the temple and taking them away. Others gathered around the real—damn it!—Uriel, perhaps in an effort to save him.

He wanted to help, but he didn't have a place there. He didn't even think his assistance would be appreciated, judging by the way Raze had pushed him aside.

He was so lost in self-pity that he missed the approach of the new presence until the sound of a cleared throat drew his attention. Looking up, he found himself facing one of the cyborgs who had participated in the attack on the temple.

"Hey," the strange cyborg greeted him. "Are you all right?"

For a few seconds, the fake Guiding Light stared at the other man. He remembered the cyborg's name now. Uriel had called him Logan. What did Logan even want with him? Why hadn't he stayed at Raze's side?

Hoping Logan would just go away, he shrugged. However, the cyborg couldn't take a hint. "Do you have a name?" he inquired.

The Guiding Light opened his mouth, ready to explain his identity to this ignoramus. But then he realized the cyborg had a

148

point, and the question hadn't been mocking or teasing. "Not one of my own," he replied, suddenly unable to look at the other man. He didn't have anything of his own, not a history, not memories, not even unique genes.

"Well, is there any name you'd like us to call you?" Logan inquired gently.

Logan's words struck him like a punch in the gut. He didn't know what it was about them, but suddenly he realized something important. He might not have a past, but that didn't mean he wasn't a person with an individual soul.

Uriel hadn't called him a clone, but a brother. Uriel had entrusted him with his last wishes. And while that hadn't worked out, it didn't mean he couldn't have a future, one where he'd make his own choices and memories, one where he could help his brother in every possible way.

"My name is Noah," he replied. Getting up from the stone, he said, "Let's go. Uriel probably needs us."

Chapter Ten

August 10, 2461

THE MACHINE steadily marked the heart rhythm of the patient in the cyber tube. Raze watched the face of the man trapped inside, hoping against all hope to see a sign of consciousness. As usual, none came.

Uriel seemed deep in sleep, his chest moving steadily as his lungs pumped air. His hair was shorter now, chin length, a consequence of the ordeal he'd gone through. Other than that, he looked just like he had on the day Raze had first met him, like an angel. Unfortunately, he was a lost angel, one with very little to no hope of finding his way back.

Preliminary tests said that Uriel's chances of ever opening his eyes again were 1 percent, if that. Even if, by some miracle, he did recover, he would never be the vivacious man Raze remembered.

Against all odds, Uriel had survived the explosion of the Temple of Genesis. When Raze had found him in the ruins, he'd thought his lover dead, but luck, fate, or God was on their side. Even if Uriel should have been killed by the blast, a part of him still clung to life. Even so, according to their medical equipment, Uriel was brain dead, and the only thing keeping him alive was the cyber tube, very similar to what Raze's father had once used.

Every single day without fail, Raze came here and waited for any sign of improvement. He had every intention of continuing to do exactly that until Uriel returned to him.

Pressing his hand to the thick glass, he said, "You know, baby, things are getting better. Noah's taken over the Council, and we actually have representation there now—my father and Hugh. Abigail and the others are behind bars, where they belong. A new headquarters for the regime is being built, not a temple this time around. Logan and Julian are looking into creating a serum from Noah's blood, one that will help every cyborg in the world regain the use of his implants."

It hadn't been easy, but as it turned out, purist citizens had been outraged upon learning of the methods the Council had used to clone their Guiding Light. That had made it possible for Raze to imprison the former Council without actually publicizing their real crime. In fact, it was probably fortunate that Uriel's clone had taken to calling himself Noah, asserting that he was Uriel's brother, never his replacement, because otherwise, things could have gotten even messier.

There had been those who questioned Uriel's legitimacy as the genuine Guiding Light due to his relationship with Raze. At that point, Raze had stepped in and pointed out Uriel wasn't a tool, but a person who deserved to love and be loved. He'd unveiled all the filth hiding behind their facades of nobility, the information Logan had gathered since inventing his VR club. After that, no one had been so eager to throw stones.

"All evidence of Project Uriel is gone now," Raze continued, "and that's for the best. I think the whole of Eden would be destroyed if the truth about it ever came out. But I wish you knew.... You weren't to blame, baby, not really. You were only a victim."

Still no answer. Raze released a heavy sigh, wishing he knew how to make Uriel react. "I miss you so much, baby. I can't believe you ever even thought that I'd mistake your brother for you."

As if summoned by Raze's words, Noah slid into the room and approached the cyber tube. "How is he?"

Raze continued to stare at Uriel and studiously avoided looking at Noah. "The same. My heart tells me he's still in there somewhere, but…."

Noah put his soft hand on Raze's shoulder and squeezed. Raze wanted to shove it off, because the hold reminded him far too much of Uriel for comfort. Hell, even being in Noah's presence had become a burden. Raze couldn't bear seeing Noah so vibrant and alive while Uriel lingered in his comatose, vegetative state.

His lover's brother almost seemed to guess his thoughts, because he whispered, "Raze, look at me."

Raze couldn't ignore Noah, so he complied. Facing Noah felt like a punch in the gut, but he pasted on a small, meaningless smile. "What is it?"

Noah brushed his fingers—those slender, white fingers that were just like Uriel's—over Raze's lips. "Don't push me aside," he said, leaning against Raze.

His body felt just right against Raze's, and yet everything else about the embrace was all wrong. Raze broke free of Noah's hold, shaking his head. "Don't do this, Noah. Please."

"Uriel's last wish was for us to be together," Noah argued. "Let me help you."

Noah had told him that before, the night of the explosion. The memory of that attempt still pissed Raze off, and it certainly didn't help that Noah was trying again, right here, next to Uriel's cyber tube.

"He's not dead," he spat angrily. "Don't speak like he is. You can't replace him. No one can."

"I know that," Noah answered, his eyes filling with tears. "But Uriel wanted you to be happy. I feel like I'm failing you and failing him. I couldn't help him in the temple, and now...." His fists clenched and unclenched as he breathed in deep gulps of air. "He called me his brother. He never saw me as a clone. But he wanted me to take his place because he loved you beyond everything else, and I need to fulfill that last wish."

Just like that, Raze's anger melted away. "Oh, Noah.... You can't. No one but Uriel can make me happy. I think, in his heart, Uriel knew it too. He was too worried about me not to try."

Noah opened his mouth, looking like he wanted to say something else. Before he could do so, the door slid open and Julian walked inside. "Hey," he mouthed at Raze. "Logan wanted me to let you know something's wrong with the VR engine, and he wants you to check it out. I'll stick around to watch over Uriel if you need me to."

Raze frowned. He wished he'd have been able to read Julian's tone, but unfortunately, Uriel had been unable to help Julian, as Julian's problem was one of brain damage, not implant malfunction.

Of course, the last thing Raze wanted was to look into Logan's VR, but the engine remained an important tool even now, after it was no longer used to exploit the perversions of the purists. "Thanks. I'll go check it out." Turning toward Noah, he added, "Think about what I said. You have your own path. You just need to find it."

Without waiting for a reply, Raze left the room. Their new headquarters were larger and more luxurious than the one under the junkyard, so it took him far more time to reach Logan's new and improved workshop. The moment the door slid open, he immediately addressed his friend. "What's up?"

"I'm not sure, really," Logan answered. "I've been getting the strangest signals off the VR module. It's like someone's accessing the Guiding Light program from a remote location without my permission. I thought I was being paranoid, but just now, someone loaded an old VR session."

Logan turned on a monitor, and Raze found himself looking at an image of his own little meeting with the VR Uriel. "What the fuck?" he asked. "Who could be doing this?"

"I have no idea," Logan replied. "I couldn't trace the signal. I tried entering the VR myself, but I didn't have any luck, so I was hoping you could try."

"Of course," Raze replied, still staring at the images. He'd probably been a bastard too, because he'd used the engine to exorcise his lust for Uriel, and maybe he deserved having that exposed. But he didn't want Uriel's image dragged into further filth.

He lay down on Logan's sofa, and his friend proceeded to outfit him with the VR goggles. "I'm truly not sure what to make of these readings in the VR engine," he said again. "I simply can't track them to a root source. If someone has tech that can scramble my devices, it could be a problem."

"Don't worry," Raze said darkly. "I'll track it down."

"Good luck."

Logan booted up the VR engine, and suddenly Raze ended up in the very same room and on the very same bed where he'd once found out that no, he couldn't replace the genuine Uriel with an illusion. That illusion faced him now, inches away from him, completely naked, like he'd been in the original VR session.

"Hi, Raze," the fake Uriel said softly.

Raze crawled away from Uriel, glaring at the stranger. Someone was obviously using the shell of the VR module to address Raze. The fake Uriel didn't sound like the coy seducer Raze had once taken to bed.

"Who are you and what in the world are you planning?"

"Do you really not know who I am?" the other man asked quietly.

A sudden realization hit Raze like a ton of bricks. "U-Uriel? Baby, is that you?"

Uriel nodded, offering him that smile, that beautiful twist of lips that Raze hadn't seen in anyone else—not even in Noah. "I'm still not sure what happened after the bombs exploded, but one of the scientists at the Temple was a regular user of this VR module. When I connected with the systems to detonate the missiles, the shock trapped my mind here."

No wonder Uriel had been brain dead. His consciousness remained in the VR engine. To think that Raze had almost convinced Logan to shut down the VR altogether. Shit.

Unable to control himself, Raze pulled Uriel into his arms and hugged him close. Even if they were both naked, the embrace held nothing sexual. It was all about comfort, about acknowledging that they were together once again, that death hadn't won out.

Raze hadn't held Uriel since three months earlier, when he'd first found Uriel in the ruins of the temple. At that time, Uriel's body had been covered in third degree burns. The wounds had been treated since then and had all but disappeared—but Raze hadn't even gotten the chance to kiss Uriel once before his lover had been inserted in the cyber tube.

He fixed that now, brushing butterfly-light kisses all over Uriel's face. Uriel melted against him, and in spite of the fact that they were in the VR, his scent and his warmth felt impossibly real. "Sometimes I could hear your voice," Uriel whispered, "but it was so distant. I don't know how it happened, but maybe it guided me here."

Raze had always felt that some part of his lover responded to his speaking. Logan had told him it wasn't possible, but Raze had disagreed, and it seemed that he'd been correct.

Breaking the embrace, Raze gazed deeply into his lover's eyes. "You have to come back now. We can be together again, just like we wanted."

Uriel's lower lip trembled, and he seemed a step away from crying. "I... I don't know if I can. Wasn't my body destroyed in the blast?"

Raze shook his head. "You suffered serious injuries, but you miraculously survived. You've been in a coma for three months."

"So that's why you never believed my brother was me." Uriel smiled, but the expression held guilt and sadness. "I could feel that you didn't."

Raze's heart twisted with fear and uncertainty. "I wouldn't have ever mistaken him for you, baby. You're the one I love."

"Oh, Raze...." Uriel clutched Raze's arm so hard it hurt in spite of the VR safety protocols. "I didn't come here to stir that pain. I wanted.... We never got to say good-bye. Everything happened so fast, and I made so many mistakes. It was unfair of me to ever ask my brother to pretend to be me. But I think, Raze, that you can still be happy. Even if I'm not there, you can find someone else to love. My brother was a bad choice on my side, but anyone would be lucky to have you."

Raze hated the resigned sadness in his lover's voice. "I don't need someone else. We just have to connect your body to the VR engine and we'll have a way to bring you back."

For a few moments, Uriel looked at him without speaking. At last he smiled sweetly. "Perhaps," he said. "But first, Raze... I want you to touch me. One more time."

Raze wanted to chase away each and every one of Uriel's uncertainties, and he leaped at the chance to do so. He pressed his lips to Uriel's, telling his lover without words that he would not allow their separation. At first the kiss was gentle, more of a tender lip-lock really, but it quickly grew fervent. Uriel's sadness shattered into a sensual despair that echoed within Raze, demanding that he claim his lover on the spot.

And maybe it was a bad idea. Maybe he should have looked into awakening Uriel first. But his heart refused to abandon this moment of closeness. After three months of clinging to a spark of desperate hope, he finally had Uriel in his arms, and he couldn't let go.

He thrust his tongue into Uriel's mouth, groaning as his lover's flavor hit his taste buds. It was just like he remembered it—no, better. The uniqueness of Uriel's spirit had translated his physical essence into this virtual realm, all for Raze to worship with his touch. The aroma of Uriel's surrender drove him wild with lust, and every thought beyond his need for his lover disappeared in a shower of electrical sparks.

As he ravaged Uriel's mouth, Raze pushed his lover down on the silken sheets. He could only be thankful that they were both naked—courtesy of their resuming the session Raze had started months earlier. This way there were no barriers between them, no uncomfortable limitations on what they could do. Raze covered Uriel's body with his own, and as if on cue, Uriel arched against him, releasing one of his trademark whimpering moans, which Raze eagerly swallowed within his kiss. It went to Raze's head, and to his cock, with the intensity of a sudden thunderstorm.

Uriel's dick insistently nudged Raze's hip, obviously as excited as Raze's own member. Biting down on Uriel's lower lip, Raze snaked his hand between their bodies and gripped both of their pricks. The generous amount of precum made the glide easy and oh-so-delicious. As their shafts slid together, Raze's urgency began to increase more and more. His testicles burned with the need to come, and his skin sizzled with that familiar energy that only Uriel could summon forth.

Raze tore his mouth away from Uriel's, because as much as he enjoyed his lover's taste, it no longer felt enough. In fact, nothing would suffice except burying his dick inside Uriel's body.

Even as he pulled away, though, a part of him ached to prolong the moment. He took in the expanse of Uriel's body with greed and no small measure of despair. Somewhere at the back of his mind, he still remembered a time when Uriel's now-smooth cheeks had been unrecognizable under the trace of burns, when his hair had been scorched by the blaze of the explosion. Here in the VR it was just as long as it had been once, the day Raze had met him.

His hand trembling, Raze reached for those long tresses and kissed them. It was something he'd seen countless believers do when Uriel had been considered just the Guiding Light, but for him, it meant more.

Uriel seemed to realize that, because he cupped Raze's cheek with a gentleness that had nothing to do with carnality. He didn't say anything, but he didn't have to. Raze could see the beautiful emotion in the emerald of his eyes.

He pressed a kiss to Uriel's palm, then to each individual finger, never looking away from Uriel's beautiful face. Somehow he ended up sucking Uriel's digits in his mouth, at which point, the tenderness melted into desire again. Before he knew it, Raze bent over Uriel and sucked Uriel's nipple into his mouth.

Uriel gasped, falling back against the pillows and starting to writhe under Raze. Encouraged by his lover's reaction, Raze reached for the other pink bud and tweaked it lightly with his fingers. Uriel didn't delay in reacting. "Please!" he cried out. "Please, take me."

The breathless sound of Uriel's voice broke Raze's mind. He released Uriel's nipple from his mouth with a wet pop, then traced the lines of Uriel's abdomen with his tongue until he reached his lover's belly button. In spite of the desire rising to maddening heights within him—or maybe because of it—Raze couldn't resist the temptation of wiggling his slick muscle inside the tiny hole.

"Raze!" Uriel screamed. "P-please... I need...."

Uriel trailed off, apparently unable to continue, but Raze knew exactly what his lover needed. Without any word of warning, Raze progressed lower down over Uriel's body and took Uriel's dick in his mouth.

At this point, Raze was too far gone to attempt gentle ministrations. He bobbed his head up and down Uriel's cock, devouring him, needing to taste his seed—even if it was only in VR. Uriel thrust erratically into Raze's wet cavern, and his hands landed in Raze's hair, perhaps trying to anchor himself or making an attempt to guide the rhythm. Raze went along with it, groaning at the evidence of Uriel's desire. When the vibrations made Uriel shiver in distressed arousal, Raze increased the strength of his suction, hollowing his cheeks as he demanded Uriel's offering.

Of course the proximity of Uriel's ass tempted him too much. He reached between the perfect globes of Uriel's asscheeks, rubbing one dry finger over the tiny hole hidden between them. Just like that, Uriel erupted, filling Raze's mouth with his seed.

Raze gulped down every single drop of Uriel's essence, knowing the sweet nectar could easily become his addiction if he wasn't careful. Hell, he almost came simply at tasting it, and he only managed to keep himself from doing so because of his need to be inside Uriel.

As he licked Uriel's dick clean, Raze watched Uriel ride the waves of his climax. Uriel was so beautiful in his pleasure that Raze wanted to give him more, to show him more, to be more, all for him. Already with a tentative plan in mind, he flipped Uriel onto all fours.

He expected Uriel to have some trouble with supporting himself in this new position, but he'd clearly underestimated his lover. Uriel pushed his ass out, offering himself to Raze. With a nearly angry growl, Raze spread Uriel's cheeks, exposing his hidden opening. Since they were in VR, Raze could have just thrust inside without fearing hurting Uriel, but he didn't. Instead he buried his face between Uriel's cheeks and tongued the rim of Uriel's hole.

Uriel dissolved into incoherence. Whatever pleas he'd uttered before now became a series of keening cries that more than encouraged Raze. Using his slick muscle like a little cock, he stretched his lover, tasting him in the most intimate way possible.

Uriel moved back against him, fucking Raze's face, demanding more, demanding everything Raze had to give. Raze tried to keep a hold on his control. Really, he did. But he was and would always be crap at denying Uriel. In the end he could no longer prolong the torture—neither his nor Uriel's.

He lifted his head, temporarily abandoning his ministrations on Uriel's sinfully beautiful ass. He spat in his palm and slicked up his cock—something that was largely unnecessary given that his precum pretty much provided him with the lubrication he needed. Truth be told, he could have probably found an actual lube dispenser, but he didn't have the patience or the focus to move away from Uriel.

His lover didn't seem to mind. In fact, judging by his wiggling, he just wanted Raze to get on with it. At last Raze surrendered to the inevitable and positioned his dick at Uriel's hole. Slowly, ever so slowly, he slid home.

For the longest time, Raze remained completely motionless, and this time not because he didn't want to hurt Uriel. Rather, he suspected that if he moved, he'd embarrass himself by coming far too soon.

The possibility of embarrassment became irrelevant when Uriel tightened his asscheeks around Raze's dick. Raze snapped. Fortunately, it didn't translate to his foiling his own plan through a premature ejaculation that would have mimicked their first time together. He pulled almost all the way out of his lover, until only the head of his dick remained inside. Then he shoved back into Uriel's channel with so much power that he almost propelled Uriel forward into the headboard.

At the last moment, he stabbed his hand into Uriel's hair, burying his fingers in the silken mass and holding on tightly. He wrapped his other arm around Uriel's waist, supporting the younger man. And okay, maybe it wasn't solely for Uriel's benefit. Maybe he just really liked touching Uriel's hair and holding him close. Whatever the case, his lover responded beautifully.

Uriel's ass greedily welcomed him in, squeezing him like a tight, velvet fist. Burying his face in Uriel's hair, Raze inhaled deeply, beginning a slower, softer pace. He was careful to find Uriel's prostate with each of his motions, and his efforts were rewarded by an increase in the volume of Uriel's cries.

Not only that, but everywhere his body came into contact with Uriel's, Raze felt electricity crackling between them. At one point, the image of the VR session began to shift, undoubtedly due to the unleashing of Uriel's enduring power. He obviously still possessed a great deal of his peculiar abilities, and Raze's body, mind, and soul couldn't help but respond. Every time Raze brushed his dick over Uriel's prostate, tiny bursts of energy exploded over him too.

Under the circumstances, Raze couldn't hope to keep his desire for Uriel in check. Tightening his hold on Uriel's hair, he started to thrust harder in and out of his lover's sweet body. He kept moving, increasing the pace, trying to get deeper, always deeper. He desperately needed the friction, the delicious heat between them, and the rising ecstasy, but he was almost afraid to pursue his desires, lest this moment have to end.

Alas, Raze could not resist the ruthless demands of his body and Uriel's. It certainly didn't help that Uriel met him thrust for thrust, apparently as wild with need as Raze himself. They fell into an unrelenting pace, moving in complete synch with one another like longtime lovers. Heat, desire, energy, lust, love, despair—a million emotions and sensations came together, some Raze's, some Uriel's, some shared. The intensity of it was quickly propelling Raze toward orgasm. The unbearable pleasure sizzled in every atom of Raze's being, and yet Raze didn't want to come. Not yet. Not just yet. Never, if it meant having to leave Uriel's body, having to release him from their deep embrace.

It was a paradox, one that had Raze writhing, torn in the blaze of feelings and fears he could no longer deny. In the end, it was Uriel who made the choice for him. He whispered one single word, and his husky murmur struck Raze like a ton of bricks—in an entirely good way.

"Raze," Uriel said. A simple syllable, four little letters—the sound of Raze's name on Uriel's lips, and Raze was a goner. It could have been because in his heart, he'd thought he'd never hear Uriel say his name again, especially not in this way. Or perhaps a possessive part of Raze that reared up whenever he took Uriel responded to the sound. Whatever the source, the results were the same. Thrusting one last time inside his lover, Raze came, filling Uriel with his seed.

Remarkably, even if Uriel had come once before, Raze's climax triggered another wave of pleasure within the younger man. With a cry, Uriel arched against Raze and exploded as well. A shower of sparks filled Raze's vision. Suddenly the world grew bright, impossibly bright. Raze convulsed through an orgasm that threatened to take away his very sense of identity. Uriel's power seemed to short-circuit and reboot him over and over, throwing him into a stream of pure ecstasy that he could hardly comprehend.

And then... it all ended. The VR engine cracked under the onslaught of Uriel's energy. Propelled out of the dream, Raze opened his eyes to find himself on Logan's couch again.

As he tore off his goggles, he looked around the room, trying to figure out what had happened, or rather how he could fix it. Logan was currently busy trying to extinguish a fire that had consumed a good part of the computer mainframe he'd used to create the engine. "What the hell happened, Raze?" he asked. "The VR is gone."

Gone. His one way to connect with Uriel, lost. Crushed with grief and despair, Raze didn't answer. He just sat there, wondering how things could have turned out like this—and if Uriel had anticipated it all along. It certainly explained his lack of interest in discussing the possibility of his return.

Raze struggled to his feet, forcing himself to take a deep breath and not hyperventilate. It was okay. They could fix the VR. They'd find a way to bring Uriel back. He refused to accept the alternative.

He was about to approach Logan with this tentative plan when Julian burst into the workshop, breathing hard. One look at his brother told Raze more than he needed to know. "What happened?" he asked nevertheless.

"It's Uriel.... He just flatlined. The cyber tube stopped working, and then Noah collapsed."

Raze almost threw up. He almost short-circuited right then and there, his mental computer refusing to accept Julian's words. He remembered the quiet way Uriel had asked to be touched and saw what it meant now. Uriel had been telling him good-bye, and Raze had been too wrapped up in his own foolish desires to realize it.

In a daze, he left the workshop and headed toward Uriel's medical room. There were already other people gathered around, trying to make the machines work. Noah lay on a nearby couch, thankfully still breathing, but as far as Raze could tell, Uriel's chest wasn't moving.

It occurred to Raze that, without the machines working, the cyber tube didn't provide any oxygen to Uriel, or any sort of life support for that matter. Maybe it was that realization or pure grief that made him punch straight through the reinforced glass. Careful not to send any shards over Uriel's body, he removed the breather and all of the devices that had once helped Uriel stay alive.

Finally he pulled his lover out of the cyber tube. He wanted to attempt resuscitation, but before he could do so, Uriel took a deep breath. All of a sudden, his eyes opened.

"Well, that was unexpected," he said.

At the same time, Noah stirred on the couch. He rubbed his temple and grimaced but seemed otherwise unharmed. "Oh, my…. Do I even want to know what that was?"

Raze stared from his lover to Noah, then back to Uriel. He wanted to scream, to cry, to ask, to pray. Nothing but a choked grunt came out. Obviously, the shocks Uriel had been giving him ever since they'd met were sabotaging his ability to think.

Nevertheless, Uriel replied to his unasked question. "Yes, Raze. I'm alive. You can kiss me now."

Raze did exactly that. He pressed his mouth to Uriel's, and the same kiss that a few minutes ago had exploded into a passionate coupling now tasted of tears, uncertainty, and relief.

When they broke away, Raze finally found his voice. "H-how?"

"I think you know how," Uriel replied. "The AI of the VR engine was consuming me, and I reached out to you with the last of my power. And then we…. When you touched me… it triggered something, and I got propelled back into my body."

Raze had actually thought that, through his lust, he'd destroyed his only chance to have Uriel again, but apparently things had been the other way around.

Noah chose this exact moment to interrupt. "Welcome back, brother," he said, patting Uriel's shoulder. Nudging Raze, he added, "Oh, and Raze... Do warn me the next time you plan to do something like that. Uriel and I still have a connection."

"There won't be a next time," Raze piped up. He brushed his fingers over Uriel's cheek, still in awe that he could touch Uriel again. "I'm counting three different occasions you nearly stopped my heart, baby," he told Uriel. "And I might be a cyborg, but my heart is very human. No more."

Uriel smiled at him, leaning his head on Raze's shoulder. "Well, you know what they say. Third time's the charm. I'm back for good."

In Uriel's voice, Raze still heard a hefty dose of guilt and sadness. It couldn't be helped. Uriel's past carried too many scars, too much pain for it to magically disappear.

But just as Raze's love for Uriel had brought him back, it could also heal those wounds and make Uriel see what a beautiful person he was. As their family and friends all surrounded them, cheering, Raze set himself a new life's mission. He had his Guiding Light back, and from now on, he'd show Uriel that, no matter what happened, their love would always be pure.

Epilogue

URIEL STARED into the mirror, absently passing a brush through his now chin-length hair. He kind of liked the way it looked. He'd never realized how much of a burden it had been. Then again, many things about his position as the Guiding Light had weighed on him terribly. Perhaps his hair had been a symbol of that.

Raze stepped up behind him and wrapped his arms around Uriel's waist. Uriel met Raze's concerned eyes in the mirror. "What?"

His lover squeezed him tighter in his embrace, as was his way recently. "Are you sure you're ready for this? You can still take more time to make a complete recovery."

"I know," Uriel replied, "but I'm not just doing this for them. I'm doing it for me too. Noah is trying, but he needs my help and my support. And I owe it to Eden, and to the world, to fix the mistakes the Council made."

Raze frowned, and Uriel couldn't say he was surprised. On that point, they would never agree. Raze firmly believed that Uriel couldn't be blamed for the deaths that had occurred when the so-called virus had struck. Objectively speaking, Uriel knew he was right. He'd been only a baby, not even aware of what was happening and what had been done to him.

But when he'd been scanning the files on Project Uriel, he'd seen the exact calculations that had led the Council to create him. He knew how many cyborgs with a dangerously high CC had existed at that time and how many had died. Raze's father had been among the lucky ones—if spending twenty years as a vegetable could be considered luck.

Even when he told himself that he'd only been the tool of the Council, Uriel still realized he had a serious responsibility to the entire world. Raze must have known he couldn't change Uriel's mind, because he didn't insist. He kissed Uriel's temple and said, "All right. But just know that I'm always by your side."

Hand in hand, Uriel and Raze left their quarters. Ironically, the large structure where they lived had once belonged to Ezekiel Zion—Uriel's biological father. Uriel had never actually been here before, which was a good thing, because it meant he'd only have good memories of it.

The mammoth building consisted of a two-story mansion with three different wings. Many members of the cyborg resistance had moved in pending renovations to the ghettoes, and a whole wing was occupied with research equipment.

As Uriel and Raze descended the stairs, they ran straight into Noah. Unlike Uriel, he'd kept his hair long, which was a good thing for people who couldn't have otherwise told them apart. Noah kissed Uriel's cheek and took his free hand in his own.

"Ready?" he asked.

Uriel tangled his fingers with those of his younger brother. "As ready as I'll ever be, I guess. You've been doing this for longer than I have, though. Is it that brutal?"

"It was worse in the beginning," Noah replied, "but things are pretty much up and running these days. Still, I only know most of these people through implanted memories, so your input will be valuable."

"Don't sell yourself short," Raze offered. "Without you, this whole thing could have easily turned into a disaster."

Noah smiled shyly, and Uriel squeezed his brother's hand tighter. It was true. If Noah hadn't been there as a figure to follow, Eden could have easily descended into civil war after the destruction of the Temple of Genesis. As it was, things were still pretty unstable, but already getting better.

Of course, that didn't mean Edenian citizens were about to forget him anytime soon. The moment they left the house, he saw them waiting outside, beyond the tall fences. Most of them cheered, but there was a group that started to boo.

Uriel threw a glance their way, but Raze urged him to keep walking. "It's hard for some people to adapt. Don't worry. We're watching them so that they won't actually cause trouble."

A hovercraft pulled in, ready for them to get on. Logan stepped out of it, waving cheerfully. "Greetings, Your Holiness," he said teasingly. "I'll be your chauffeur today."

Since Uriel's recovery, Logan had become quite friendly to him. Noah had told Uriel once that Logan felt terribly guilty about his original treatment of Uriel. Uriel had decided to act like it had never happened. In the end, Logan had been entitled to have his suspicions.

Still, he didn't want to use his old title, and he decided to point that out. "You can simply call me Uriel," he answered with mock haughtiness. "And yes, I will allow you the honor of escorting me to my destination."

Raze released a disgruntled sound. "I thought I was your escort."

Noah and Logan both snickered, and Uriel proceeded to pacify his lover by pressing a brief kiss to his cheek. "You're so much more than that."

He didn't mean it as a joke, and he didn't take the gesture lightly. He wanted everyone to see and realize how important Raze was to him, and that their relationship would never be up for debate. Throwing one last glance toward the group that didn't seem so happy with his recovery, he made a mental note to approach them. It was a good thing that Raze had allowed them to express their opinion, but Uriel needed them to understand that they were all in this together, and that with cooperation, they could build a better, stronger Eden.

Together with Raze and Noah, Uriel entered the hovercraft. Logan slid into the pilot seat and started the vehicle. It seemed so strange and alien for Uriel to travel like this—before, he'd only used carriages pulled by horses. Yet another thing that had changed. For some reason, it made Uriel smile, and it encouraged him more than he'd have thought possible.

They reached the new Council headquarters in record time. The building was still being erected, but its glass and metal structure looked completely different from the stone temple that had once stood in its place. The agora remained as wide as before, but a monument had already been built in its center. Raw, simple, and sleek, it depicted the abstract figures of two men, one of them made of stone, the other made of metal. A child lay at their feet, crying as she stared at her stone and metal hands. Somehow the image managed to capture everything Uriel felt about his role in the decimation of cyborgs.

"Do you like it?" Noah asked as they left the hovercraft. "I wanted to make something that reminded us all of the mistakes of the past—so that we wouldn't repeat them."

Uriel nodded wordlessly. He should have known his brother had been the one to create it. He was probably the only one—other than perhaps Raze—who would ever understand the burden they'd always have to carry. Then again, only the two of them, Raze and Logan, knew about Project Uriel, with the exception of its creators, of course.

They walked past the monument and into the Council Headquarters. Raze led them into a meeting room, where the new Council members were already waiting. Raze's father, Lucius, was already there, as well as Lucius's friend, Hugh Wells. So were Phelps and a few other former members of the purist regime.

Uriel had heard that his former butler had become one of the staunchest supporters of the new political system. Having seen Uriel being taken away, he had known the Council members were lying and had narrowly escaped with his life.

Phelps smiled when he saw Uriel. "Welcome back, Your Holiness. It's an incredible relief to see you well."

"Please, call me Uriel," Uriel replied. "I think we've gone past that stage in our lives."

They all sat down around the table, and for a few moments no one spoke. It seemed that none of those present had expected Uriel to return from the proverbial dead. They weren't ready to handle it, because on the one hand, Uriel argued he didn't want to be treated as special, and on the other, he'd survived an explosion that would have killed anyone else.

"Let's get to the point," Uriel said. "As some of you might know, my brother and I have a form of bioenergy, an ability which we gained through genetic engineering. That ability allowed me to survive the incident at the Temple of Genesis, and it can also help us improve our international and domestic standing."

"I'm not sure we have to focus on international issues right now," one of the former purists said. "We still need to rebuild. The eyes of the entire world are on Eden. People take their cues from us, and our treatment of cyborgs will automatically begin a change."

"That's true," Uriel answered, "and we've already made a difference. And now my brother tells me that he's been looking into creating a serum that will reboot the implants of everyone who's suffered in silence throughout the past decades."

"Such a serum would be taxing financially," Phelps argued. "We could not simply give it away."

Uriel grimaced. Just the thought of taking money for a cure they owed the world made him sick to his stomach. But Eden was struggling and would likely continue to do so. People were used to cyborgs doing all the work for next to no pay, and the change had forced them to face new realities. Everything from the educational system to healthcare needed to be completely overhauled.

So far, cyborgs had agreed to continue to work in the factories, but their world was changing, and past policies were no longer valid. Noah had made sure abuse of cyborgs was no longer legal, but it was not enough. Not to mention that the rest of their country still hadn't gotten the answers they needed.

"Has there been any reaction in other Edenian cities?"

"There've been some riots, but nothing major," Hugh replied. "We've dispatched troops from the capital to ensure safety."

"On that note, I have to disagree with my esteemed colleague on the matter of international affairs," Lucius piped up. "We're already receiving messages from Gallia and Iberia demanding answers. Ships of cyborgs are sailing toward us from Europe, some of whom have already demanded political asylum. We have to help them, but…."

He trailed off, and Uriel finished his phrase for him. "But their presence will create more political instability and will be a challenge for our food and energy supply."

"Even if we did have a serum," Lucius added, "it would be unlikely that other countries would even purchase it now. They're more liable to dump their unwanted citizens on us than change their own ways."

"Let's not exaggerate," Phelps argued. "In most countries, anticyborg sentiment isn't nearly as aggressive as in Eden. We've always given the cues. Besides, most will want the use of their implants back."

"Not if there's the slightest chance that it will backfire again," Raze replied. "It'll be a long, laborious process, and there's no way it'll happen overnight. I can't imagine they'd even be inclined to trust us right now."

"You're right," Uriel said with a sigh. "Rushing into creating the serum won't help us. We need to start at the beginning and stabilize Eden. We have to establish a budget and a clear plan on reforming the legislation. One step at a time."

Everyone seemed to agree with that idea, at least at first. It soon became obvious that most of the people here had clashing opinions, and they couldn't reach unanimous consent on the extent of the changes that needed to be made. By the end of the meeting, Uriel had a terrible headache and was just realizing that the burdens of decision making could weigh even heavier on him than his previous responsibilities.

They did manage to make some progress, clarifying the legal stature of cyborg workers. They couldn't confiscate the properties of former members of the purist regime, but they did establish a heavy tax on fortunes that had been earned through the sweat and abuse of cyborgs—money that would be pooled into the ongoing renovations of the ghettoes.

At the end of the meeting, Uriel felt both satisfied with what they had achieved and frustrated that he couldn't do more. He thanked the Council members and left the building filled with more questions than he'd had before.

"Don't be so down," Raze told him, obviously detecting Uriel's displeasure. "We can't fix everything all at once. If we even make the attempt, we'll botch it."

"I know," Uriel replied with a heavy sigh. "There's just been so much pain already. The knowledge that we have the cure within our grasp and we can't deliver it kills me."

In morose silence, they bypassed Noah's monument and slid inside the hovercraft. "Where to?" Logan asked. "Back to the house?"

Uriel shook his head. "I want... I heard you're keeping the former Council members jailed. I want to see them."

No one argued. Logan started the hovercraft and headed out of the city. He followed the exact same path he'd once used to take Uriel away from his gilded cage, which made sense given that the prisoners were being held at the compound that had once been Uriel's so-called home.

It was so strange to relive everything that had happened, to see the pastures around the compound as green as ever. Even the hill where Logan had once collapsed their escape craft had recovered from the fire. It gave Uriel a measure of hope, and it also made him wonder if all this land couldn't be put to better use. Agriculture needed to flourish more if they planned to rebuild Eden.

Before Uriel could consider that idea too closely, they reached their destination. Logan flew the hovercraft into the underground hangar. Uriel waited until the aircraft AI gave them the all clear, then undid his safety belt and slid out of his seat.

Once again, Raze took his hand as they made their way out of the hovercraft. Memories assaulted Uriel, and with every step he took, he squeezed Raze's palm tighter. It made him more aware of why he'd been there and why he'd existed at all. Would that guilt ever fully disappear? Probably not.

Every corridor reminded Uriel of things he'd done, wishes he'd made, dreams he'd had. He recalled even now that day when he'd found the romance novel his mother had destroyed. The library was just around the corner, perhaps with hundreds of other treasures waiting to be found.

"The books…," he said softly.

"I had them moved," Noah said. "They're kept in a special section of our HQ now. You can look them over when you have time. I know I do."

Uriel shared a smile with Noah. He'd never truly understood how much of his memories Noah had borrowed. Cloning was a difficult, unstable process, which was why it had been outlawed in the first place. The recollections Noah did have had been artificially implanted. Nonetheless, he liked that his brother had chosen to make his own memories. It soothed some of his guilt over asking Noah to replace him in Raze's life.

"Are you okay with being here?" he inquired.

Noah nodded. "I've visited the compound before. It's… a bit strange. I don't feel like the Guiding Light, and maybe I never did. Being here hammers that home."

"Just like I said," Raze piped up, "you have your own path."

Before Noah could say anything else, they descended into a part of the compound Uriel had rarely visited. It had once been meant purely as a storage area, but apparently it had been reshaped to add individual cells.

Uriel walked past the temporary homes of Ezekiel Zion and the rest of the Council members without stopping. He ignored their calls and kept going until he and his companions reached Abigail's cell.

His mother walked up to the energy bars that kept her trapped in her tiny square of assigned space. "Hello, Abigail," Uriel greeted the former councilwoman. "I see you're doing well."

"Not as well as you," the woman answered. "Release me at once, Uriel. You have no right to keep me here. I committed no crime—"

"I can't believe you even have the audacity to say that," Logan interrupted her.

"And what exactly did I do?" Abigail inquired with a sneer. "Tell me. I'm waiting."

Uriel didn't speak, and not necessarily because he didn't want to give her the satisfaction. Truth be told, they were in the unfortunate position of not being able to truly punish Abigail and the others for what they had done. If they wanted to do so, there would have to be a public trial. Everyone would learn of the true causes of the virus, and the rest of the world would rebel against Eden.

It made Uriel feel filthy and guilty, like he was hiding the dirty secret his so-called parents had kept for decades. Abigail must have guessed that, because she snickered. "You can't even say it. You know that if it comes out, your precious new political regime will collapse like a castle of cards. Tell you what? Release me, and I won't start shouting it to the winds."

"You can't exactly do that from here, can you?" Raze leaned in closer to Abigail, and something in his fierce expression made her back off. "And you did commit countless crimes. You attempted mass murder by planning to launch the missiles against the ghettoes.

You cloned Uriel—when you know very well cloning is illegal. You tried to kill Phelps and all the staff at the compound who knew Uriel had been taken. You tortured and abused Uriel for years before I even showed up."

In his heart, Uriel couldn't consider the cloning a crime, because he already shared a bond with Noah. With his free hand, he once more reached for his brother in a silent gesture of support. Noah smiled tremulously but said nothing. Uriel wished he'd left Noah behind in Genesis.

Seeming completely oblivious to the exchange, Abigail glared at Raze. "You're not listening to me, cyborg. If you don't let me go, I will reveal Project Uriel to the world."

"Uh-huh," Logan replied. "That's an empty threat and you know it. You like to be alive too much."

Abigail's nostrils flared with obvious frustration. She turned toward Uriel again and said, "Uriel, please reconsider. You must realize that I only wanted the world to recover from the spiral of destruction it was headed into. You have to understand. I'm your mother, and—"

"We share genetic material," Uriel interrupted the woman. "That doesn't make you my mother. You were never a parent to begin with, not really."

It was true that she and Ezekiel had provided the basis for the genetic project they'd seen Uriel as, but that meant nothing. Yes, a long time ago, he had craved Abigail's affection. She was the only one who'd ever touched him or been close to him in any way, before Raze had shown up. Maybe he'd come here for some closure, and maybe he'd had questions. Why would she create Project Uriel in the first place? Why kill so many? Did she even feel any remorse over it?

Seeing her like this answered that dilemma. She still thought she'd done the right thing. She thought that the world had needed the culling she'd orchestrated. Hell, she'd never even addressed Noah at all—even though Uriel's brother had been there the whole time. Undoubtedly, she considered him a lower life-form. It sickened Uriel.

174

"I have only one regret now," he added. "That you might not ever be punished the way you deserve. But you will never, remember this, never get out of here. If you even make the attempt, you'll find that your guards are just as well trained and trigger happy as the ones you once commanded."

"Do you think that will change anything?" Abigail exploded. "Do you think keeping me and the others imprisoned will magically fix all your problems? You might have great abilities, Uriel, but Eden is far too large for you—and you'll never be able to reach out to everyone."

Something clicked in Uriel's mind as he took in her words. "That's it," Uriel said, turning toward Raze. "That's what I have to do. I have to travel through Eden, reach out to our citizens, empower them, reassure them, heal them."

In the cell, Abigail burst into laughter while Raze blinked in surprise. "Travel all throughout Eden? Baby, that'll be tremendously taxing on you."

"I know," Uriel answered, "but I can do it, Raze. You know I can. And the rest of our citizens deserve the chance to have their pain taken away. As long as there's a discrepancy between how things are in Genesis and the rest of Eden, none of our carefully laid plans are going to work."

"You're right," Noah offered, speaking for the first time. "I can stay here and work on the legal part, but you'll be doing more if you truly reach out to people. Still…. Are you sure you're up to it? You've just recovered from your coma."

"I have a new chance," Uriel told both his brother and his lover. "I won't waste it. This is my purpose, I know that now. The people still look to the Guiding Light for help—and I will provide it, but as Uriel. As a man."

From the cell, Abigail said, "Uriel, you can't rebuild anything from a lie. The secrets you keep will be your downfall."

Her warning no longer held any smugness or any threat. For once she sounded serious, and that made Uriel look toward her.

175

"Perhaps. And maybe one day someone will learn of it and will come after me. But if that is the case, I want my legacy to be the rebirth of our world, not more pain and suffering." He leaned closer to Raze and kissed his lover's cheek. "Unlike you, I have love to rely on."

TWO WEEKS after Uriel's recovery from his coma, he and Raze left Genesis for their extended trip throughout Eden. Their family saw them to the edge of the city, where their transport vessel was already waiting.

His heart heavy with anxiety and teeming with hope, Uriel pulled Noah close. "Good luck," he said as he hugged his younger brother one more time.

"To you too," Noah replied, embracing Uriel just as fiercely. "We'll keep in touch. I'll miss you."

"And I you."

Noah shook Raze's hand more sedately, likely aware that Raze still felt a measure of discomfort around him. Uriel's recovery was gradually clearing away the awkwardness, and Raze had understood that Noah had only approached him out of the desire to fulfill Uriel's last wish. However, it was too soon to completely forget. Uriel blamed himself for making the unreasonable demand in the first place. He could only hope the distance would be good for them all and that it would give Noah some time to find his own soul mate.

Raze embraced his brother and father, who'd naturally also come to see them off. "Consider that surgery," he told Julian. "You can have your voice back now."

Julian just shrugged and mouthed, "I have all the time in the world to focus on myself. There are other more important problems we have to deal with."

"Family always has to be the most important thing," Uriel reminded him. On a whim, he embraced Julian as well. They hadn't gotten the chance to spend much time together, but Uriel knew how much Julian meant to Raze.

Meanwhile, Raze sighed, apparently resigning himself to the inevitable. He squeezed his father's shoulder and said, "Take care of yourself."

"That's my line," Lucius replied. "Watch your back, Raze, and don't forget to let us know if you run into any kind of trouble."

Finally, Raze clutched Logan's hand, then pulled his friend into a tight embrace. "Good luck, my friend," Logan told him. "And be happy."

"I am," Raze replied. "I have Uriel, remember?"

With that last good-bye, Raze and Uriel got on their hovercraft. It was a long-distance transport vessel, larger and more comfortable than anything Uriel had used before. Uriel immediately rushed to the observation deck, a sort of bubble on the side of the hovercraft that allowed passengers to watch the scenery during flight. Uriel didn't care much about the scenery now, but he did want to see his brother for a while longer.

Noah and the rest of the group had already stepped back to give the aircraft space for takeoff. Even if it felt a little childish, Uriel waved at his brother, and Noah waved back. He pressed a hand to his chest, repeating once again what he'd told Uriel outside, "I'll miss you."

Uriel hated being forced to leave his brother, but it couldn't be helped. Finally the engines of the hovercraft started. Raze pulled Uriel away from the observation deck and buckled him into his seat. As he took position by Uriel's side, his hand landed on Uriel's, and he squeezed it tightly. With their fingers entwined on the armrest, Uriel said, "Thank you for being with me, Raze. I don't think I could have done this without you."

"Maybe, maybe not." Raze kissed his cheek and smiled. "But you're the one we owe everything to. Whatever happened in the past, we can rebuild what was lost. I believe that, and I believe in you."

"In us," Uriel amended.

The hovercraft finally took off, and that temporarily interrupted their conversation. Uriel had been a little nervous at having to fly with such a big vessel, but it didn't feel much different from his previous trips. If anything, it was far smoother, the aircraft obviously more resistant to air currents and turbulence than the ship the cyborgs had used for their escape.

Once the hovercraft settled at a certain flying height, Uriel freed himself from his seat belt and returned to the observation deck. Genesis had already disappeared into the distance, and as far as the eye could see, there were only fluffy white clouds and blue skies.

Uriel wanted to see it as a good omen, but for some reason, the farther they went from Genesis, the more uneasy he felt. He tightened his hold on the banister while Raze wrapped his arms around him. "I'm worried, Raze."

"I know you are, baby," Raze replied, kissing his ear. "But I'm here, and I won't allow anything to happen to you, ever again."

Raze's words and familiar scent comforted Uriel. He relaxed in Raze's arms, staring out into the distance and taking in the peacefulness of the moment. He was doing the right thing, and he had Raze. What could possibly go wrong?

The speed of the aircraft allowed them to reach their first destination in less than an hour. While Genesis was by far the largest city in Eden, there were other settlements that held many citizens and offered many of the supplies needed to run Genesis. The first of the towns in question was Zion. As the name illustrated, it had been founded by loyalists to the House of Zion, which was why it was important for Uriel to reassure them.

The hovercraft was greeted with outstanding enthusiasm in Zion—at least from the citizens. That wasn't wholly surprising, since Uriel had never traveled here before, and some people couldn't afford to make the journey to Genesis or to wait for hours on end to see him.

Changing the way they saw him would be a problem, but one that would have to wait. For the moment, Uriel and Raze needed to face the Edenian official in charge of the area. The governor, Abraham Zion, was already waiting for them when they descended from their aircraft, but Uriel didn't kid himself into believing this would be easy.

"Greetings, Your Holiness," Abraham said. "It's a great pleasure, no, an honor to receive you in our city."

"Thank you, Governor," Uriel replied. "We appreciate your hospitality. I'd like you to meet Raze Hartman, my Guardian and partner."

It wasn't an ideal description of what Raze meant to him, but they hadn't discussed marriage, and Raze needed to be introduced as something. Abraham grimaced—a fleeting expression that Uriel might have missed altogether if he hadn't been watching for it. "Zion welcomes you, Mr. Hartman," he said. "We appreciate all the efforts you put into making sure our Guiding Light lacks for nothing."

Uriel didn't miss the hint of sarcasm in that phrase, not shocked in the slightest by the attitude. After all, Abraham was a distant cousin of Ezekiel's. Within the first minutes of their meeting, it became obvious that the governor hated Raze. By noon, Uriel was fairly certain the governor didn't like *him*. By evening, he was wondering if he could find any tactful way to ask for a food tester. Abraham was liable to poison him. There were sneering comments and disgusted looks, mostly directed at Raze but also at Uriel.

Uriel kept his temper in check and for the most part ignored the governor. He approached the people instead. He gave so many speeches his throat went raw, and he organized a larger assembly for the following days. All the while, the governor kept haunting him like a malevolent shadow, throwing in little sarcastic digs that made Uriel grit his teeth in frustration.

It was late that night that Uriel finally snapped. He and Raze were about to return to their quarters when the staff notified them that a different room had been assigned for Raze, in an area reserved for cyborgs.

Furious, Uriel found the governor in his lounge. "I won't have you poison my people with your prejudice," he said as he burst through the door. "I came here to spread a message of peace and unity. I understand your loyalty to the House of Zion, but I am its leader now, not Ezekiel. You owe me respect, and if you can't give me and my Guardian that, you will be removed from your position."

Abraham sneered. "You can't threaten me. You're only a child who thinks he's won the war without realizing it was only the first battle."

"Each and every day is a battle," Raze shot back. "You are a battle, and we have many others ahead. But if you're not with us, you're against us."

"Don't even talk to me, you machine. If you think that just because you're fucking—"

Energy shot out from Uriel's fingertips, cutting Abraham off before he could finish the insult. Abraham released a soft cry and collapsed to the floor, twitching, his eyes rolling in his head.

Uriel managed to stop the power before it could do any permanent damage, but even as Abraham tried to crawl away, he himself fell to his knees. What was wrong with him? He never lost his temper or snapped at people like this, and he never used his power to hurt others, not outside life-and-death situations.

Raze knelt next to him and hugged him close. "Are you all right?"

Uriel took a couple of deep breaths and shook his head. "I don't think I am. Something's wrong, Raze. I can feel it. We need to go back home."

WATCHING HIS brother leave was among the hardest things Noah had ever done in his life. Not that he'd had too many experiences throughout his own existence, but that was beside the point.

Even as he squinted at the sky in an attempt to track down the aircraft Uriel had departed in, a deep, heavy uncertainty filled him. He felt bereft, without an anchor. The only other time he'd experienced this emotion was when Uriel had been in a coma.

180

And just like then, Logan showed up by his side. He pressed his hand to Noah's shoulder, distracting him from his glum thoughts. "Hey. It's all right. They're perfectly safe, and what they're doing will help Eden a great deal."

Noah turned toward the cyborg but didn't answer. He did know that Uriel's idea was for the best of all Edenians and perhaps the world, but neither of them could be sure if Uriel and Raze were truly safe. A great deal of resentment and concern had flooded Edenian cities, and while Uriel and Raze had guards with them, something bad could always happen.

Nonetheless, Logan's encouragement and his familiar smile helped. Noah even found himself smiling back, and for the most part, all throughout the rest of the day, he didn't fall into morose musings again. But that night, when Noah retreated to bed, he had a nightmare. It started, of course, with Uriel and Raze. He dreamed of their hovercraft crashing, of their bodies consumed by fire, scorched and broken like Uriel had been once before.

And then the dream shifted. Suddenly he heard Abigail Zion's accusing laughter. He saw her standing in a field covered in corpses, holding a bloody knife in her hand. "You can't do anything to stop me," she told him. "You're too afraid."

Over and over, those words repeated in his head. The figures of children hovered around him, fixing him with sightless, dead eyes. Metallic arms and legs fell on top of him, followed by human skulls. Suddenly Noah was swimming in blood, so much blood. It was in his mouth, in his lungs, choking him, keeping him from breathing. Cracked mirrors danced around him, displaying distorted figures of him, or maybe of Uriel. Noah didn't even know anymore. He couldn't think. He couldn't speak. He could barely even scream.

But he did scream, and he woke up shouting the house down as he hit the floor of his bedroom. It was still dark, and the holowatch on his nightstand told him it was a little past midnight.

Getting up on shaky feet, Noah made his way out of the room. He slipped on the staircase, still dizzy and nauseous, but kept going. A breath of fresh air and a glass of water, and it would all go away.

"Are you all right?" a sudden voice asked from the darkness.

Noah yelped and jumped back—and probably would have broken his neck by falling had Logan not caught him. "Careful," the cyborg said. "You'll hurt yourself."

Still trembling, Noah nodded. "I just had a nightmare," he replied tightly.

Logan hummed thoughtfully and guided Noah downstairs. As if he'd known exactly what Noah had been thinking, he took Noah outside and placed him on a bench. He retreated into the house, then returned moments later with a glass of water.

Noah greedily drank down the liquid while Logan watched him in silence. Finally, when Noah set the glass aside, Logan asked, "Want to talk about it?"

Noah considered the question and shook his head. Out of everyone he could have approached about his nightmare, Logan was likely the least appropriate person to discuss it with. Yes, from the very beginning, he'd been nice to Noah, and Noah desperately wanted to cling to him. Other than Uriel, Logan was the only man who made him feel... real, like a person in his own right. But Logan had also lost his entire family twenty years ago. Uriel's involvement in it still weighed heavily on all of them, always the elephant in the room.

"I don't think I can," Noah replied, unable to hide his regret.

"Fair enough," Logan said. "You know, I don't blame Uriel anymore. For what happened, I mean. And I certainly don't blame you."

Noah wondered if he was truly that transparent. He decided it couldn't be very hard to guess the reasons for his guilt and finally asked, "Truly?"

"Yes," Logan answered, staring into the distance like he wasn't addressing Noah at all. "It's a heavy burden to carry, this secret, this pain. I don't think it will ever truly go away. But it's not his fault, and definitely not yours."

Instead of studying Logan's sharp, masculine profile, Noah followed the other man's gaze, scanning the horizon. The stars glittered with cold beauty, and Noah asked himself if his brother and Raze were looking at them too. What about Logan? What did he see when he looked out there? Were there any answers to the questions Noah couldn't ask?

Silence fell between them, thick with doubt and apprehension. At last Noah got up from the bench. "Thank you, Logan," he said quietly. "Your words mean a lot to me."

It was easy. So easy. He waited until Logan retreated to his room, then sneaked outside. Stealing the hovercraft didn't pose any sort of challenge, and neither did reaching his destination. He knew the way to the compound, and his power had been growing steadily the more time he spent around Uriel. After that, it was only a matter of disarming the security systems and sneaking inside. The cyborg guards were a bit harder to bypass. Noah thought he might be able to briefly shut them down, but that would automatically draw attention to the one person other than Uriel who could do that—him.

In the end, he found he didn't have to actually go inside the cells. Focusing on the computer systems was enough. Sparks of electricity flew from the energy bars of the cells and onto the former Council members. They didn't even scream. Their eyes rolled in their heads, and they fell to the floor, dead, the voltage shutting down their hearts. A small fire in the living quarters kept the cyborg guards distracted long enough for them to miss the little episode.

When he was done, Noah returned to his hovercraft and flew back to the house. He couldn't say he was completely surprised when he found Logan waiting for him.

"What did you do?" Logan asked, narrowing his eyes at Noah.

Noah didn't answer. He didn't know if Logan would be angry or not. He realized that the Council members' deaths would be a problem, but he simply couldn't let them get away with it—not when he still heard the crying, the screaming, not when he still felt the pain.

He gave the cyborg a pleading look, hoping Logan would understand. Logan released a heavy sigh. "Come with me. This will be our secret. You never left, and you spent all night in my room. Got that?"

Noah just nodded and followed Logan inside. In the distance, alarms started blaring. Somewhere at the back of his mind, Noah heard his mother's voice saying, "The secrets you keep will be your downfall."

ALANA ANKH is a hopeless romantic. Once upon a time—no, not in the Stone Ages, but when Alana was a nosy teenager—she lived and breathed mainstream romance, but after she discovered m/m.... Well, her fate was sealed.

Regardless of the genre, Alana thinks love can be painful, heartbreaking, but also fun, corny, and a little silly. Love is different for everyone and anyone—and in her books, she tries to celebrate that.

Alana also loves sci-fi, fantasy, and paranormal. But even if her boys have scales, fur, claws, fangs—or whatever else occurs to her—they're really very nice people. Most of the time. Well.... Most of them are nice, but all of them deserve love and a HEA.

When Alana isn't feeding her addiction to happily-ever-afters and hot men, she's randomly slaying monsters in MMORPGs or thinking up the next idea to share with readers.

You can find Alana at http://alanaankh.wordpress.com/ or on Facebook (which she does try to monitor) at https://www.facebook.com/alana.ankh.

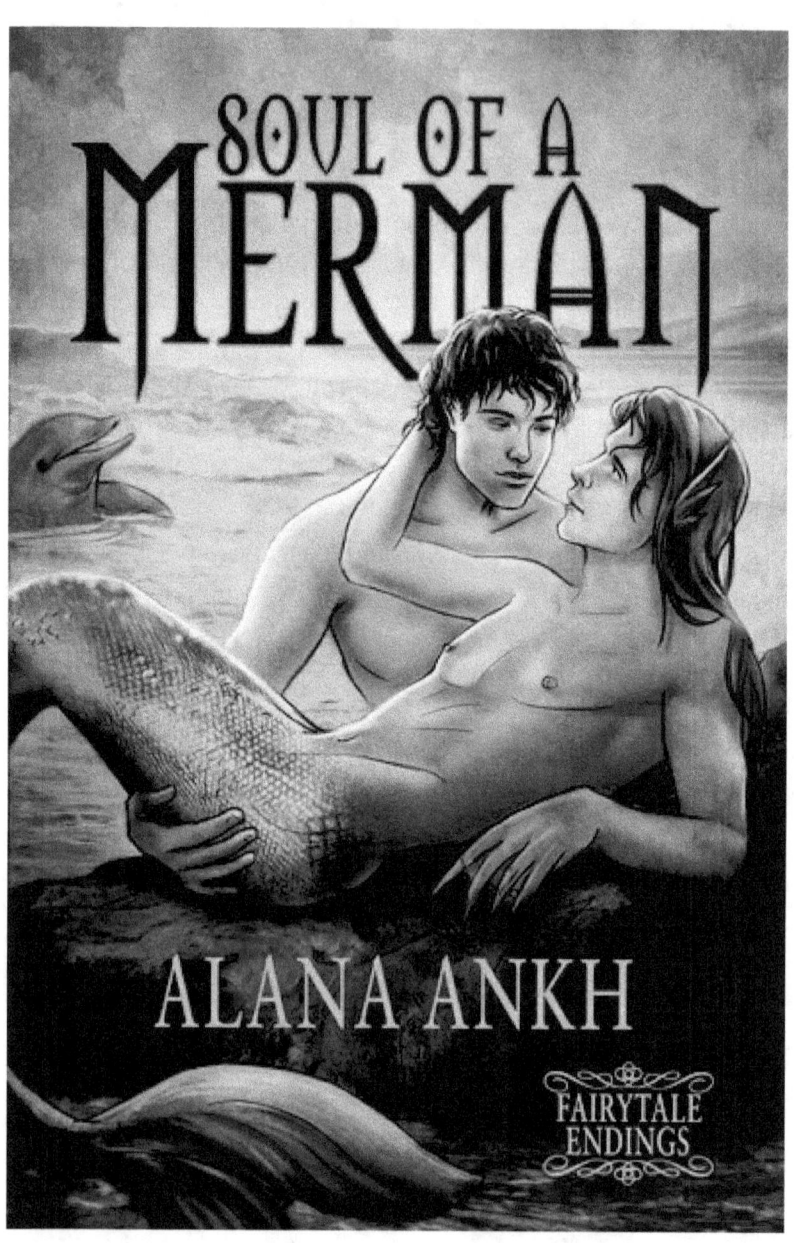

SOUL OF A
MERMAN

ALANA ANKH

http://www.dreamspinnerpress.com

GRAVITATIONAL ATTRACTION

ANGEL MARTINEZ

http://www.dreamspinnerpress.com

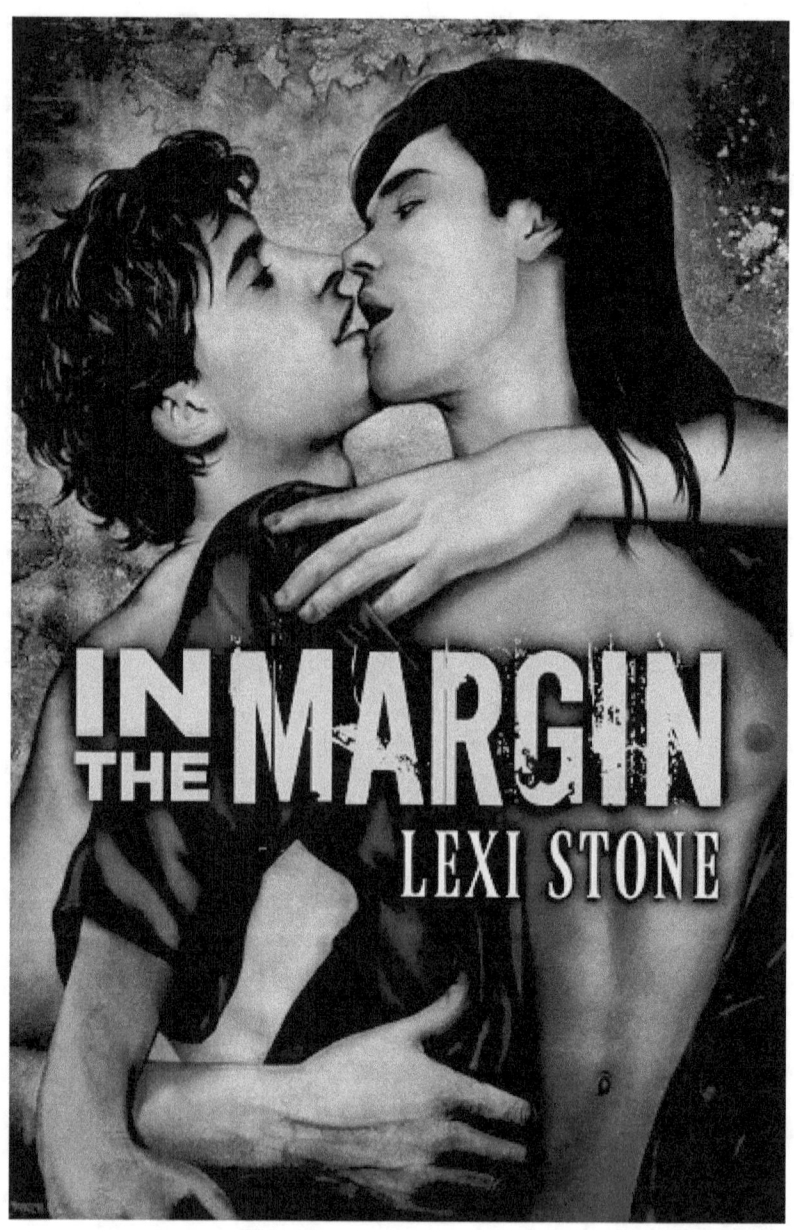

IN THE MARGIN

LEXI STONE

http://www.dreamspinnerpress.com

ESCAPE FROM CONICA

ROBERT CUMMINGS

http://www.dreamspinnerpress.com

BE MY ALIEN

MOONLIT SKIES

M.A. CHURCH
JULIE LYNN HAYES

http://www.dreamspinnerpress.com

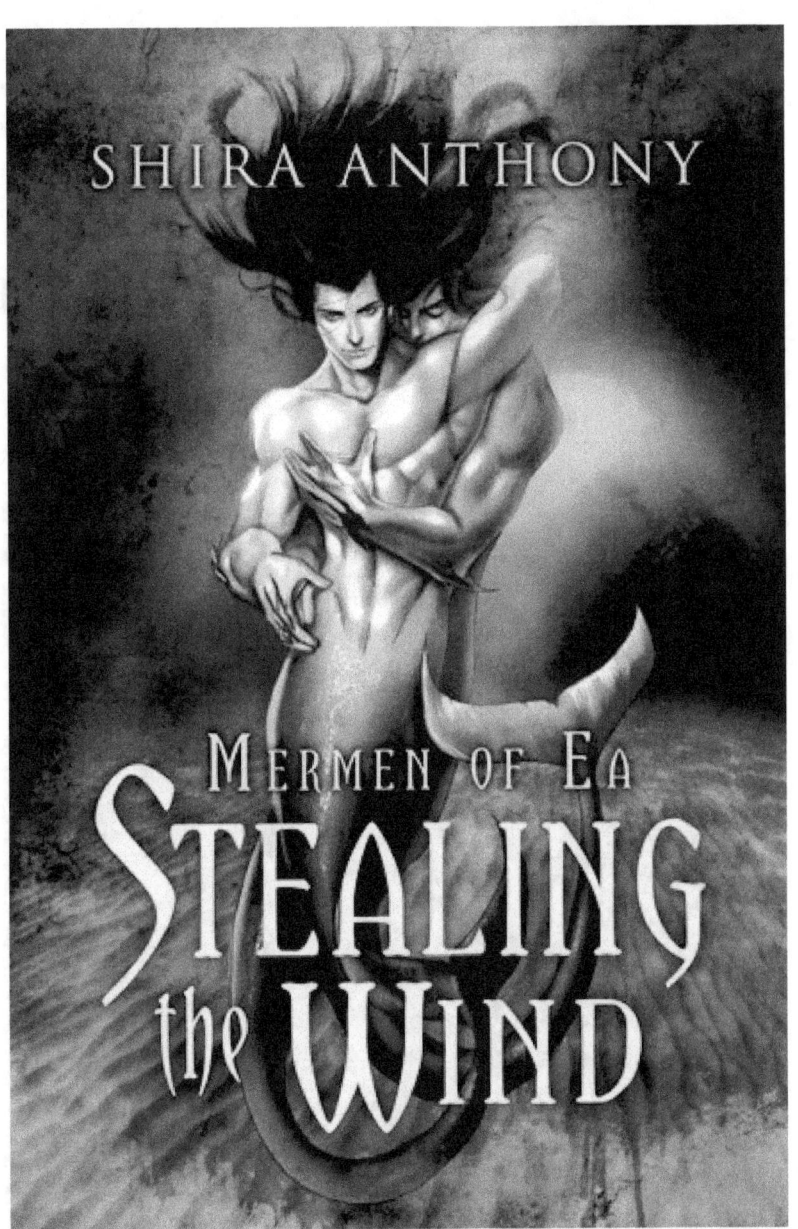

SHIRA ANTHONY

MERMEN OF EA
STEALING
the WIND

http://www.dreamspinnerpress.com

KIM FIELDING

Pilgrimage

http://www.dreamspinnerpress.com

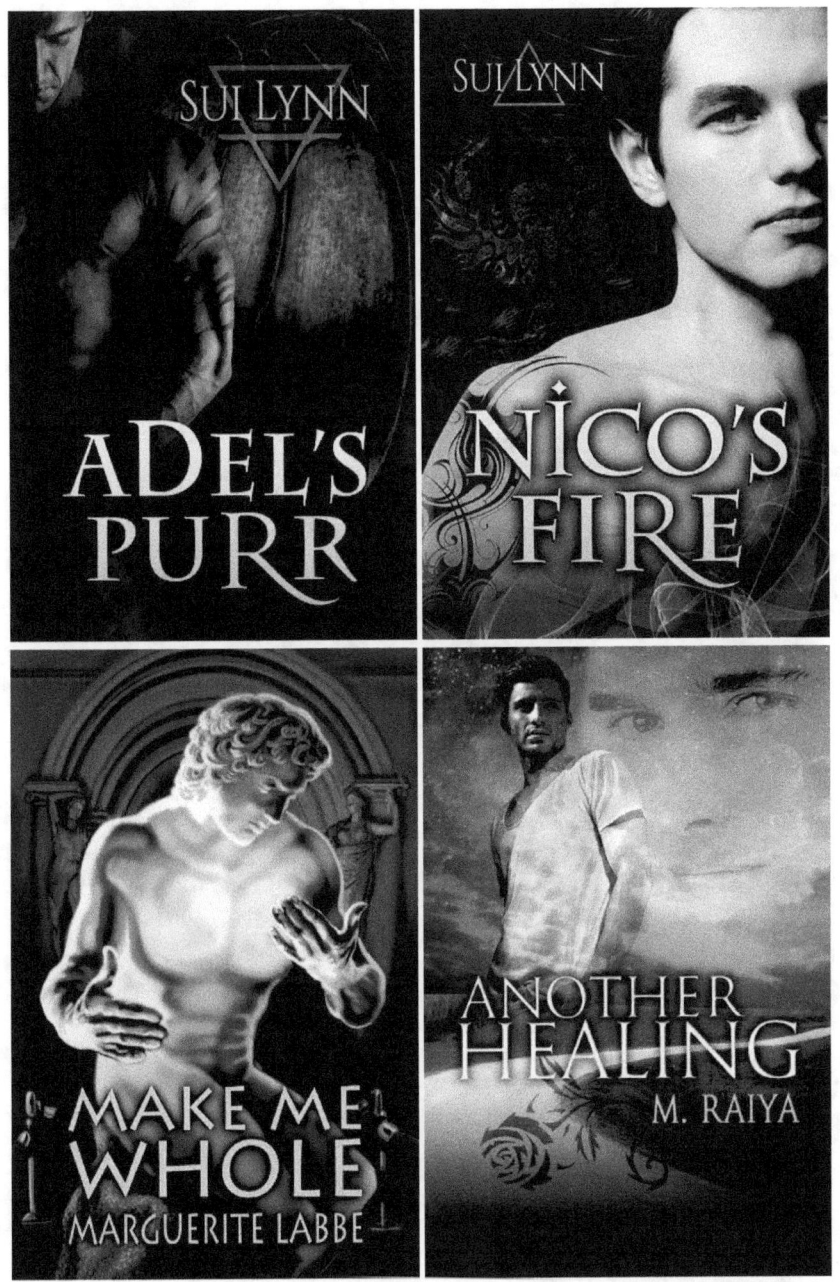

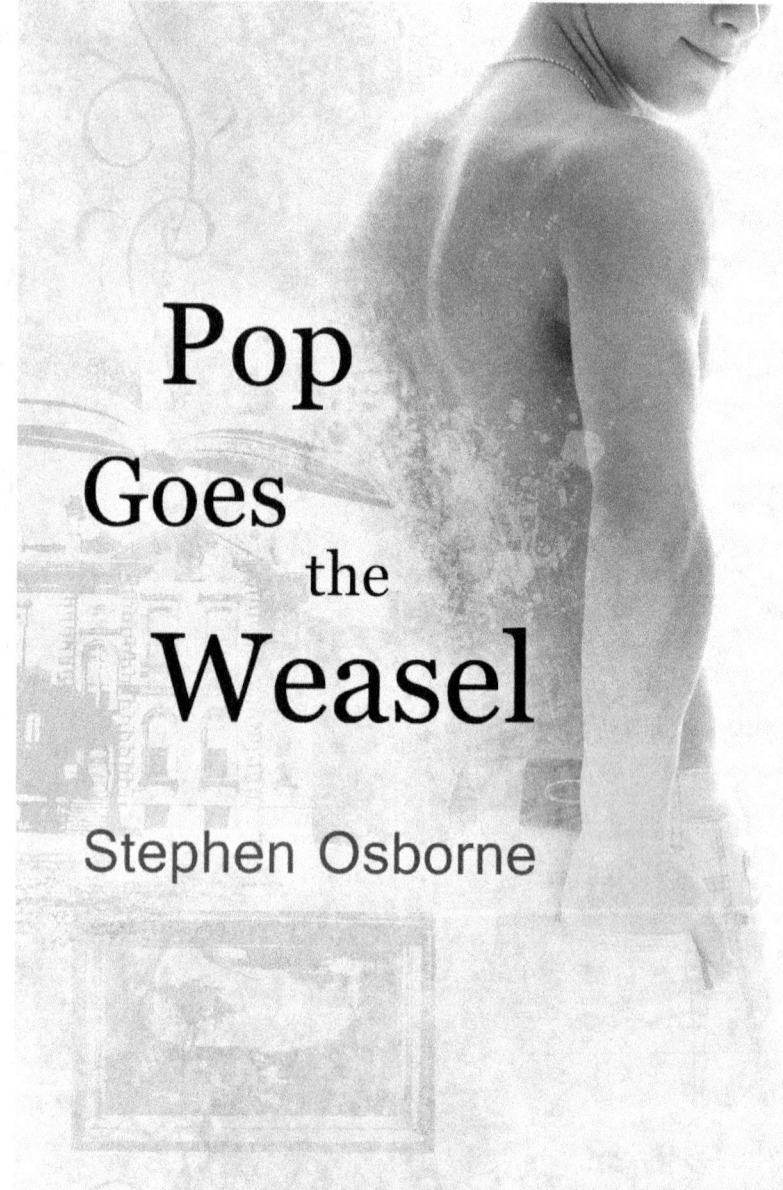

Pop
Goes
the
Weasel

Stephen Osborne

http://www.dreamspinnerpress.com

RINSE
& REPEAT

AMBERLY SMITH

http://www.dreamspinnerpress.com

www.ingramcontent.com/pod-product-compliance
Lightning Source LLC
Chambersburg PA
CBHW060058260626
47160CB00005B/1715